I0586890

Do Not
Go Alone

C.A. Larmer is a journalist, editor, teacher and author of multiple crime series, stand-alone novels and a non-fiction book about pioneering surveyors in Papua New Guinea. Christina grew up in PNG, was educated in Australia, and spent many years working in Sydney, London, Los Angeles and New York. She now lives with her musician husband, boomerang sons and their very cheeky Bluey on the east coast of Australia.

Sign up for news, views and giveaways:
calarmer.com

ALSO BY C.A. LARMER

The Posthumous Mystery series:
Do Not Go Gentle

The Murder Mystery Book Club series:
The Murder Mystery Book Club (Book 1)
Danger On the SS Orient (Book 2)
Death Under the Stars (Book 3)
When There Were 9 (Book 4)
The Widow on the Honeymoon Cruise (Book 5)
Gone Guest (Book 6)

The Ghostwriter Mystery series:
Killer Twist (Book 1)
A Plot to Die For (Book 2)
Last Writes (Book 3)
Dying Words (Book 4)
Words Can Kill (Book 5)
A Note Before Dying (Book 6)
Without a Word (Book 7)

The Sleuths of Last Resort:
Blind Men Don't Dial Zero
Smart Girls Don't Trust Strangers
Good Girls Don't Drink Vodka

PLUS
*After the Ferry: A Gripping
Psychological Novel*

An Island Lost

C.A. LARMER

Do Not Go Alone

LARMER MEDIA

Published by Larmer Media
Northern NSW
Australia
www.calarmer.com
Paperback ISBN: 978-0-9924743-4-8
Cover design by Stuart Eadie
Edited by The Editing Pen
& Elaine Rivers (with heartfelt thanks)

This one's for Charlie.

PROLOGUE

There's a bullet in my head, and it's really messing with my hairstyle. Blood is trickling through my ash-blond highlights, and there's a smattering of something egg-like caught up in my diamanté tiara, which doesn't bear thinking about.

It's a tedious thing, but I'm guessing I'm dead, and that's not even the tedious part. I've quite clearly been murdered, executed gangland style—one bullet to the noggin and a smoking gun lying on the rug beside me. Seriously. The gun still has the whiff of smoke about it.

How ridiculously cliché.

Except this shouldn't be happening to me. My name is Maisie May. I'm twenty-seven. I work for a Sydney law firm, drive a Mini Cooper, and live in the 'burbs. A different sort of cliché, I suppose.

In any case, I shouldn't be dead. I should be dusting off my midnight-blue jumpsuit, reapplying the lip gloss and heading back towards the pool, where there's a party going on. My party, in fact, and it's still going on, despite all this. Nobody's cottoned on yet. Which is a worry, right? The longer it takes, the less chance they have of kissing me back to life.

Oh who am I kidding? That bullet wound looks particularly nasty, and the way the blood is coagulating while I float above speaks volumes. The very fact that I'm *floating* at all is a dead giveaway, if you'll excuse the pun.

I'm here but not here, a ghost of myself, a carbon copy minus the carbon. *Get it?*

I feel no physical pain, in case you're wondering, and who would blame you if you were. You'll be dead eventually too. But my emotions are a little wrought, and I can still imagine my limbs and my stomach and the weight of my heavy heart, and the truth is it's getting heavier by the second. I'm starting to feel a little disappointed, a little, well, *ripped off*, to be frank. I don't want to be dead. I didn't ask for this, and I certainly didn't ask for those creepy strangers who are waving enthusiastically from the sidelines, like I've just popped out for their lunch orders.

Because yes, to add insult to injury, I can now see dead people. Terrific. This night just goes from bad to worse.

Can *you* see them, just over yonder, near that blinding light? They don't look real good from this angle. Hasn't anyone ever told them how unflattering fluorescent light can be? Perhaps if they installed a warm, diffusing lampshade they wouldn't look so garish and I might be enticed across.

Beyond the glare, there's a dark tunnel and I'm no fool. I know exactly where that leads. A feeling of dread creeps down my nonexistent spine. If my life is over—and I'm not sure I'm quite ready to accept that yet—there is no way I'm going down any dark tunnels with that mob. I don't know those people! Have never seen them before in my life.

Where's my lovely grandma? She died yonks ago. Where's Uncle Bob? Why aren't *they* here to beckon me across? I thought your deceased rellies held your hand when you croaked it, not a cast of strangers with creepy smiles. Besides, I'm not ready to say goodbye to the living just yet. The party's still pumping, and I intend to enjoy it.

Will you keep me company?

Will you hang out with me for a bit?

I know we've only just met, but I promise to make it worth your while. There's frothy cocktails down there and gallons of champagne and a table laden with party nibbles, courtesy of my guests. Granted, most of it has been demolished, but there are still some miniquiches, a few luridly decorated cupcakes (purple icing? *Really?*), and a whopping great bucket of hummus—if you can ignore the corn chips floating about like shark fins inside. And in the midst of it all, the remains of a rather gooey sponge cake that's dripping strawberry jam onto Mum's best tablecloth. A little like my blood has dripped onto the creamy carpet where I lie prostrate, a bullet wedged in my otherwise perfect head.

A sudden, piercing scream gives me false hope.

I glance back towards my messy self, but no, I'm still sprawled there utterly forgotten. It's just my buddy Tessa in the pool, screaming and splashing about. She was always such a screamer. And that's Roco, my boyfriend, laughing by her side. He sounds sinister. Do you think he sounds sinister?

I can't believe they're still swimming like they've got all night. Tessa is wearing a bikini two sizes too small, Roco in boardies so bright they could win a spelling bee. And around them, dozens of revellers laughing and splashing and having far too much fun, considering the circumstances. They have absolutely no clue I have just been murdered. Or at least they're *pretending* they don't, because if you think about it logically, at least one of them must have killed me, right?

How's that for a brain spaz?

One of my "friends" must have done me in. Notice those quotation marks? Notice the earlier puns? I was always very good at English. Better than Tessa, who used to cheat off me. Kind of like she's cheating on me now with Roco. And they think I don't know. Ha. Ha. Ha.

But let's not get distracted.

You must be wondering why I can't recall who killed me. It's a very good question. Why, indeed? When it comes to my murder I have a big black *nothing*. I recall getting a text on my mobile phone, I recall stumbling away from the pool deck and heading inside, and then I recall floating above my body having a very bad hair day.

Of course the killer could very well be a stranger, a psycho who just happened by. And now that I think about it, I do have a vague recollection of a shadowy figure, a man, yes. Something in his hands... Something strange by his side but...

Nope, sorry, it's gone.

Bit like my memory, which is shot to pieces (lol).

Why have I forgotten that last bit, the most important bit? The *whodunit* bit? Did the bullet wipe out the hippocampus? That's the memory part of the brain in case you can't remember. (Okay, now I'm just showing off.)

Or does it go deeper than that?

Is it too traumatic? Do I have amnesia, perhaps? I've heard of people who don't recall some horrific event like, say, a car accident. They're just merrily zooming down the highway and then *Bam*! They're waking up in hospital saying, "WTF?" Some don't even recall the last week of their life. Some the last year! I've heard of people who wake and don't even recognise their husband and kids. Or was that just in a movie I saw once?

Anyway, the point is, I'm luckier than some. I may be cactus, but I do recall the time leading up to my murder; it's just those crucial final minutes that are *blah*. Maybe that's why I'm still lingering here, annoying you while ignoring those weirdos at the light (because, yes, they're still there, in case you thought they'd shuffled off).

Perhaps it's not the party I crave so much as the truth. Perhaps if my memory kicks back in, I'll have a little closure and be closer to "moving on."

Will you help me do that?

Please, I implore you. Will you help me solve the mystery of my murder before I vanish forever wondering why someone I loved so much hated me just enough to put a gun to my head, pull the trigger and leave me lying all alone while they went back to their Fluffy Ducks and their sickly cupcakes and that stupid, bloody sponge cake?

CHAPTER 1

It's not my birthday, interestingly, and the party wasn't even my idea. It was Una's. Another stupid Una idea; she's the queen of them. Una Conway is an old friend from work, and by "old" I mean she's actually a year or so younger than me but we've been friends for five years and remain friends even though I've now left the job and moved back home and live on government handouts.

Una thought I needed cheering up.

"It'll be fun," she said. "Everyone'll come," she said.

And she was right about the latter, at least. Everyone did come. Everyone and their dog. Seriously, there was a dog out there, an Australian cattle dog I believe, and at least two kids last time I looked. I spotted them clambering over the pool fence earlier tonight. The little blighters. I had to screech for their mother to rescue them.

Who would bring animals and kids to a grown-up pool party? What kind of idiots did Una invite? My parents would have a fit.

They're away at the moment, in case you're wondering (Mum would have heard the gunshot; she would have come running). They're currently out the back of whoop-whoop, tending to Gramps. That's Aussie slang for "in the middle of the countryside looking after my grandfather." *He's* the one who's supposed to be dead, not me. He's just gone into palliative care, is a million years old. Well, ninety-five to be precise. It's his turn, dammit. It's been his turn for some time. In fact, it's almost my father's turn. He's a late bloomer, just turned seventy-four, although you wouldn't know it. The fact that Gramps isn't standing near that tunnel, below that horrifying light, makes me think he must still be clinging on for dear life. The lucky bastard.

Anyway, I digress.

So Una says, "Let's put the party on Facebook," like no one's ever lived to regret *that* idea. Next minute there's a hundred people here and they're wrecking the house even though we're all too old for that kind of nonsense. Most of us are in our late twenties, for goodness' sake. Mum was bogged down with two kids by that age. I was the afterthought that came much later, the "mistake," but there's no point dwelling on that now.

Back to the revellers.

We're not keen on growing up these days, have you noticed that? I blame *The Hangover*, an inexplicably popular movie series about grown men behaving badly, over and over again. It set off a chain reaction. Now no film is complete without the "drunken mayhem" scene where perfectly reasonable adults/FBI agents/beauty queens ingest enough tequila to keep the Mexican army legless, dance about like deranged idiots, destroy/shag/snort everything in sight, then dust themselves off and head back to the office/altar/beauty pageant looking sparkly and fresh, like they were sipping mineral water all night.

No wonder we have a drinking problem in the West, let alone no energy to grow up. I glance outside. That lot will be lucky to make it to the nearest toilet bowl to throw up. For now though, they're on speed dial. Someone is simulating sex with a plastic blow-up flamingo, someone else is standing on the brick barbecue, pouring shots down someone's throat. And what the hell is Mattie Constance doing with my mother's tennis racquet?

The stereo is blaring. It's been hooked up to someone's iPhone, and I'm pretty sure it's on repeat because what idiot in their right mind would play that Justin Bieber track three times?

This party has been heading south for hours, and it's almost hit the Antarctic. I did try to stop it at one point. Maybe that's how I ended up in this predicament. It's worth contemplating, I guess. I recall getting quite tetchy, I recall telling Una to clear the party out, and then I recall fighting with Roco, who told me to "just chillax, babe, you really need this" and Leslie who told me to "stop being a drama queen" and Tessa who said "She always gets like this."

Like what, exactly? What do I *always* get like? I'm not yet thirty for goodness' sake. I haven't had a chance to develop lifelong habits—I've barely had a bloody life. And now it's over because one of them decided to rob me of it so they could keep the music blaring.

Okay, that's a bit of a stretch. I don't really believe that, but I'm still a tad cranky that they're all out there whooping it up while I lie inside, hole to the head, bleeding into the rug.

Okay, deep breaths, Maisie. Get your shit together, says a voice inside my head.

A voice I haven't heard in a while.

Perhaps I should take this opportunity to set the scene. I know how these things work. It wasn't so long ago that I was writing creative essays in Advanced English class.

So here goes...

My full name is Maisie Leanne Theresa May. I live in a modestly sized McMansion on the upper north shore of Sydney. That's a pretty posh part in case you don't know, but not as posh as some. This house was once a gaudy monstrosity, complete with Fanta-coloured bricks and imposing Roman columns, but my folks bought it, rendered it, and camouflaged the cheesy columns with creeping vines.

Now it looks pleasant enough. Now it blends in nicely with almost every other house in the street. That's what we like to do here. We like to blend in. It's easier that way.

My bedroom is on the second floor. It doesn't blend in. I recently painted the walls lime green and added silk magenta curtains, knowing they clashed and not caring one bit. I have a small single bed that's swamped with throw cushions—no, really, there's so many cushions you can barely see the bed—and there's a tacky dream catcher hanging overhead, which is so *not me*. I got it on a recent trip to Byron Bay. That's a hippie enclave to the far north of Sydney that's actually full of hipsters and tourists pretending to be spiritual. The hippies left a decade ago. They could no longer afford the skyrocketing rents, and their hovels have since been turned into "rustic getaways" on Airbnb. I guess it's hard to afford anything when your main source of income hasn't yet been legalised.

So I bought the dream catcher. I don't know why. Maybe I thought it'd provide some answers. It certainly failed to do that.

You might be wondering why a twentysomething is still perched in the family nest, but it's not that unusual, not in modern Australia at least. Almost half of us now live at home well into our twenties, either because we have it too good and can't imagine ourselves in a rat-infested share house, or we have it too bad and can't afford a share house, even the rat-infested ones, especially if we're also hoping to save enough to put a deposit on that overpriced rat's nest.

I fall into neither of those categories, however. I'm a returnee, what they call a "boomerang kid." I did move out at the first chance I got, but then I lost my job, and well, what choice did I have? I've only been back six months, but it feels like six years. My mother clearly has dementia because she's completely forgotten my age and is treating me like a ten-year-old. Insists on doing my washing. Cooks me mushy meals. Looks alarmed every time I leave the house.

My father just stares at me glumly. I think he's

disappointed. He's always been a man of few words, but since I moved home he's become positively mute. Although he can get chatty when my girlfriends are over. He's such an insatiable flirt. They find it amusing. Me, not so much.

And as for my two brothers, Peter and Paul (yes, Peter, Paul and Maisie, and yet my parents never clicked), they just roll their eyes and can't believe I'm back.

"I'd rather kill myself," says Paul, who lives just a suburb away so really can't talk.

"I'd rather kill Mum and Dad," says Peter, who lives on another continent altogether, which, given that sentiment, is probably just as well.

So yes, we're a delightful lot.

Both my brothers were meant to be here tonight, but Paul couldn't make the party. Something about a sick kid and a cranky wife, or was it the other way around? Don't get me started on cranky Jan. Peter, who's back on holidays from his swanky London life, was here for a while, but I haven't seen him since the cake came out. He's probably snuck off to bed—and I'm not talking the lumpy mattress in the spare bedroom upstairs. Nor am I talking alone. Pete's been staying at the ritzy InterContinental. Of course. He always stays somewhere posh. I'm not sure if he's showing off to the chicks he drags back there or to us.

So neither brother is here. That's been substantiated. It's just me and thirty or so remaining guests who are in better spirits than me. *Still.*

How come no one's found my body yet? Was I this invisible when I was alive?

And how the hell did no one hear the gunshot?

CHAPTER 2

I told you how I carked it, right? A bullet to the head. How absolutely extraordinary! I mean, guns are a really big deal Down Under. Unlike some parts of the world, we don't have a lethal weapon in every glove box, undies drawer and disgruntled student's backpack. If that's not a whopping clue, I don't know what is. Although there's something about that gun... Something I should mention...

We'll get back to that in a minute. I haven't quite finished this scene-setting business, and I don't want to get you muddled up. You see I've given you the macro setting, but let's zoom right in. Let's inspect the crime scene. Let's check out the corpse!

I'm lying facedown on the carpet in my dad's study. That's just what posh folk call an office. It's a decent-sized room, with a large window that looks out to the front driveway, but the curtains are drawn and I have to wonder about that. Were they always like that, or did the murderer swish them shut? There's two doors to this study, one that's currently concealed behind the curtains and the one leading into the hallway of the house. Both appear to be closed, which helps explain why I haven't been discovered yet, I suppose.

I mean, apart from the odd stray—including Una, earlier tonight, now that I think about it—there's really no reason for anyone to wander down to this wing of the house. The office sits to the right of the front door, down the hallway, past Mum's sewing room and across from the guest toilet. But most people are probably using the facilities out the back or just urinating straight into the pool now I think of it, and I wish I hadn't.

So the study door is shut; the light is off. It's actually quite dark inside. I can barely see myself let alone Dad's desk. It's little wonder I'm yet to be discovered. Then it occurs to me that perhaps I'll lie there undiscovered for days. It's Saturday night. My parents aren't due back until Tuesday. It's a possibility, right?

I give my ghostly self a shake. No need to turn maudlin; I'm sure it won't come to that. I just hope whoever finds me is up for the job. I read once how post-traumatic stress disorder can really affect first responders. Can haunt them for life. I'm hoping it's the tall, dark, handsome stranger I was half flirting with earlier tonight. He doesn't know me, not at all. And, outside of a missed opportunity for a quick party fumble, I don't think he'd care. He certainly wouldn't be traumatised. He looks far too composed for that, with his black topknot and steel-rimmed glasses and wanky velvet vest.

For all their sins, I do hope Tessa and Roco and Una aren't the first. I'm not sure how they'd cope. Tessa's still living at home for pity's sake. Okay, that sounds a bit harsh, considering my circumstances, but I am a little different. At least I moved out once. Back when I had some purpose.

I tell people I work—*worked*—in a law firm, but the truth is I was just a lowly PA who happened to work in a law firm. It could just as easily have been a dog food factory or a bank. PA is short for personal assistant, in case you don't know, and that's a euphemism for personal slave. I located missing files and organised urgent meetings and switched schedules and fetched coffees and dashed to the nearest drycleaner when the boss's blouse got sweaty under the armpits, which it did surprisingly often, although you didn't hear that from me. I took calls and diverted calls and played pit bull at the front desk, and, well, you get the picture. I know the three partners liked to *think* they ran the show, but deep down we all knew—the partners, the clients, the accounts people, the guy who brought the muffins—that I kept the curtains open and the music playing. They may have been the balls, but I was the juggler, if you'll excuse the sloppy metaphor.

I loved my job. Really loved it. And I was bloody good at it. Before.

I have a distant memory of a cup smashing on the polished concrete floor, of eyes wide and horrified, all gasping at me...

I shake it off. That's beside the point. We have a mystery to focus on.

So, the doors and curtains are closed, that's confirmed, but my dad's office computer is switched on and is lending the room an ominous flickering glow. Now that's intriguing. Dad's retired and not one for the internet. His idea of a web search is to get out the insect spray. Did I switch the computer on? Did my killer?

I sneak a peek at the screen. I see a Facebook page is open, but I can't quite read the content. It's as though it's written in another language, completely illegible to me. Now that's just annoying. And, again, kind of intriguing because there's no way my dad left that page open (see aforementioned comments).

There's one more thing I'd like you to note. Dad's chair, the office chair, is not by his desk where it should be. It has been wheeled across the carpet to the internal wall and sits just below two hooks.

That makes me want to shudder. They're the hooks that once held my dad's pistol, the vintage single-shooter that now lies a metre or so from my head.

And so the plot thickens.

CHAPTER 3

Perhaps it's time to return to the murder weapon. Dad's gun. I did mention it was his, didn't I? It's lying just out of reach of my body and looks almost theatrical. Like someone has carefully placed it there. Maybe it's the mere presence of a gun that feels a little hammy. Like I said before, it's unusual to own a firearm in this country, legally, at least. There's generally two types of Aussies who possess guns—country folk and crooks. You can guess which camp my dad falls into, or I hope you can.

He's as straight as an arrow my dad. Never even smoked a joint. A country boy, originally from an outback property called Nevercloud, northwest of Dubbo (which is pretty much northwest of anywhere that matters). The property is aptly named. There are no clouds there, and I mean that quite literally. I don't think it's rained in a decade.

Dad grew up on the dusty, ten-thousand-acre cattle farm with his slow-talking, no-nonsense parents and three older brothers who wore matching moleskins, riding boots and Akubra hats like a uniform. There's just two of them left now. One brother, the aforementioned Uncle Bob, got killed in a quad-bike accident decades ago, the other scooted off to Western Australia and has never been heard from again. (I gather no one's worried or surprised.) The third, Simon, still lives on the property, but he wants out, preferably before he gets his wish gift wrapped in a shiny wooden box.

He's tired, Dad says, almost as tired as Gramps was eight years ago when they finally convinced him to hand the farm over to Simon. Gramps adored the property but was too old and too rickety to work it properly. Gee, what a nice problem to have! I recall feeling so sorry for him once. *Old? Urgh! That'll never happen to me!* And I guess I was right.

Grandpa May was installed in a stinky nursing home after that, and again, I recall smug sympathy when it happened. Now I'd settle for a urine-scented common room at Autumn Lodge any day.

Along the way, for whatever reason, Dad took possession of one of Gramps's guns. Not the old rifle he used to shoot stray kangaroos and the odd cattle dog who took a fancy to the fowl. This was a rare vintage pistol, a collector's item, more likely to have been pointed at someone's head by a feisty bushranger than a farmer living in the bush. Or at least that's what Dad told me when I stumbled upon it about six months ago. He was just standing there in his office, holding it in one palm as though weighing it up, considering his options. Freaked the fudge out of me.

Was he going to kill himself?

"No," he said, chortling like the idea was hilarious. "Just reminiscing is all. My dad got it off his dad, and God knows where he got it from. It's a beauty, hey?" He stroked the glossy wooden butt, fingered the silver inlay. "I think I might hang it up. This has good memories for me."

A *gun* has good memories? That's like choking up at the sight of a dentist's drill. That's when Dad told me about his love for the bush and his desire to go back one day and blah de blah de snore. He's leaving his run a bit late. He might be in terrific shape for his age, but he's not that far off Autumn Lodge himself. Not that he'd ever agree to that dive. I think he'd take the pistol to his own head if we ever so much as glanced at an application form.

But the point is, I knew about the gun, so who else did?

My brothers, I guess. It's the kind of thing men share with their sons, right? But I can't really see them turning it on me. We had our issues but...

As for my mates? Other than Una's little visit tonight— I will get to that, it may have some bearing—I don't recall any of them spending any time in my dad's study, and I certainly never told them about the pistol, but I guess I must have. Or maybe—and here's a whopping clue for you Miss Marples out there—maybe I took it to scare the guests into clearing out, and I don't know, someone spotted me and scared the life out of me instead. Literally, right. You got that metaphor?

I told you I was good at English. I might have written a book if I'd lived long enough. Of course no silly little murder mysteries for me. I would've written something more useful than that, a How-To book, perhaps, one bursting with handy information and facts. Or at least the old me would have done that. The new me would have struggled to get off the couch.

But I wanted to be useful once. I wanted to do incredible things with my life other than endless admin and digital filing and fetching flat-whites for frantic clients. Now my only use will be as click bait for online news sites. The very thought makes me sad.

Anyway, back to the gun. The more I think about it, the more it blows the case wide open (again with the puns!). The damn thing was hanging on the office wall, for goodness' sake. Anyone could have stumbled into the study, plucked it from its perch and wreaked mayhem on my brain.

Maybe I caught them by surprise and it went off by accident? Maybe they did it deliberately, luring me in with that text?

You remember that text I got, right? If only my memory was as sharp, I'd recall exactly what it said. If only my limbs still worked, I could reach down and pluck my iPhone from the pocket of my jumpsuit and tap on the square marked Messages. Maybe the answer rests inside a cartoonish green speech bubble.

I wonder if I can zoom in now and take a closer look. I'm still trying to determine how this whole death thing works. It's all a little random, to be honest. I can see through gabled tiles and plasterboard, but for some exasperating reason I cannot see through a flimsy cotton jumpsuit. And it's frustratingly inconsistent. I can't see through *every* wall now that I think about it. The two ground-floor toilets are out of bounds to me—not such a bad thing, I suppose—and the spare bedroom upstairs is one big black splotch. I have no idea who's in there or what's going on. Maybe that's where the killer is lurking.

It makes you wonder, right?

And if I stretch my neck, I can only see as far as the end of the street. I'm glancing outward now, and the farthest I can get is the T-intersection just past the McGee's house. After that, it all starts to fade into oblivion. I wonder if someone's smashed out the street lighting—

"*Pssst!*"

I glance up and back towards the tunnel.

Oh dear, the creepy dead people are getting more persistent. One woman is waving at me like a windsock. She has something in her hands, but I can't focus on that. All I can see are the purple shadows under her eyes, the blue tinge on her lips, and oh dear, is that drool trickling down her cheek?

"Go away!" I say irritably. "Just leave me alone."

I've seen the movies. I know what they want, but it's not my job to settle old scores or impart soppy messages to their freaked-out loved ones.

"I'm busy!" I yell back, then glance downwards just as someone calls out "Hey, is it time for speeches?"

Goodie, I think. Let's see what the living have got

to say for themselves.

I notice that most of the remaining guests are now in the pool or straddled along the sides, and there are at least four or five people lolling on the Balinese-style daybed that sits under the nearby pergola, so entwined in each other it's hard to count, and a little icky if I'm being honest. (What's Helen Thing-a-me-bob doing with Kyle What's-his-name's foot?)

"What do we want speeches for?" says someone else, Roco I realise, watching now as he downs the dregs of a South Pacific Ale.

I am crestfallen. That was one of my favourite drops. I haven't had it in ages.

"It's not Maisie's birthday," he adds matter-of-factly.

"Then why the party?" asks Mattie, now air-guitaring the tennis racquet while standing in the shallow end. If Mum saw that, she'd be livid. Imagine what it's doing to the precious wood.

"Why not?" Roco replies, but Tessa has stopped smiling.

She's looking around and frowning. "Where *is* Maisie, by the way? Anyone seen her lately?"

Well, stone the crow. Someone's finally noticed.

A few people follow her gaze while others shrug as if they couldn't care less, like it's not my house and it's not my pool and my whereabouts are irrelevant. I can't help feeling a flood of anger and despair.

It's been ten minutes, people! Maybe twenty. Wake up!

And then as if on cue I get my wish.

A cry so deafening it could wake the dead echoes through the house and out towards the pool. I glance back to my dad's study. Hottie Hodder is standing at the doorway, not looking quite so hot. His face is ghostly white, his lips agape.

I smile.

Grab your trench coats and magnifying glasses, people. It's game time.

CHAPTER 4

Fancy Jonas "Hottie" Hodder finding me. I could not have scripted it better. Jonas is a lovely guy, really, a friend of a friend. Well, maybe a little more than that. We do have some history, a certain "incident" two winters ago, so he kind of owes me one.

Good. Plus he's close but not so close he'll be too traumatised. Or at least I hope not.

Jonas (I don't use the nickname; I don't think he's *that* hot) is still holding the light switch he's just flicked on, the other hand spread weblike towards my body as though reaching out. I'm not sure if he's trying to grasp me or just hide the sight of me behind his outstretched palm, but it's a dramatic gesture. His voice is even more compelling, his cry now a raspy bellow.

"Oh God! Oh God! Oh Goooooood!"

It's a little late for divine intervention I think snippily as the revellers look around startled. Some leap out of the pool in a fluster, others appear from various parts of the house, one woman pulling her shirt down over a twisted purple bra. Oh, it's my acupuncturist friend Arabella. What's she doing half-naked?

"What's going on?" calls the first person to make it down to Jonas. It's Leslie, a work friend of Tessa's. She has an open bag of chips in her hand and halts just behind him at the office door, letting out her own cry, chips spluttering everywhere before others crowd in behind her.

And then "Jonas! Oh my God! What the hell have you *done?*"

This is Tessa, dripping wet in her bikini, one of my mum's oversized beach towels wrapped tight around her squishy belly. She pushes past them and into the study. She dashes for my body and drops down to my side, screaming the words over and over and over again.

"What have you done? What have you done? What the hell have you done?"

Jonas has both hands up now, backing out in the opposite direction but butting into stunned partygoers instead.

"I didn't do it!" he cries. "It wasn't me!"

Tessa is not hearing it. She is now cradling me in her arms, sobbing tears into my face, and crying, "My God, my poor baby, poor, poor lamb…"

As she brushes my bloodied hair back, she manages to smatter my own blood across my forehead, messing me up further. I really should be pleased by her outpouring of raw emotion, but all I can think is, *Back off, Tessa, you're messing with the evidence.*

Is she doing it deliberately, do you think? And why would she assume Jonas had a hand in my death? Is it purely because he was first on the scene, or does it have something to do with that aforementioned incident? I wouldn't have thought that was of any consequence, but let's add Hottie Hodder to the suspect list. (Have you officially started one yet? It would really help me out.)

For now, let's keep watching. It's all rather entertaining, don't you think?

Una has appeared and looks like a stunned rabbit, eyes wide, mouth even wider. That's also interesting because she's usually quite good in a crisis.

"Tessa! Leave her," says someone else. Roco again. He's also pushed through and is hovering over both of us, pulling at Tessa's elbow, but she refuses to budge.

"I'm calling an ambulance!" screams somebody.

"Don't bother," Roco mutters. "It's too bloody late."

How does he know that?

"Call the police," says someone else. Mr Tall, Dark and Handsome from earlier tonight. He's pushed past Roco and is now leaning over Tessa, one hand on her shoulder, another reaching down to feel my pulse.

I *knew* he had his shit together. I *knew* he'd be a good one to have about, although he better be careful or he'll get blood on that fancy waistcoat, which is now unbuttoned, one corner dipping precariously close to my wound.

"Why do we need the police?" demands Roco, who is sounding more suspicious by the second.

Tall, Dark and Handsome ignores him, reaches for his own phone and stabs in three zeros.

"Leave that!" he yells when someone goes to pick up the gun. "Don't touch anything. Everyone. Get back."

I don't know who died and made him boss, well, apart from me of course, but they do as instructed, the entire party of horrified revellers squeezing back out into the hallway, some still clutching champagne flutes, most soggy from their swim. Mum would have a fit if she saw them dripping on the carpet.

I spot the two children amongst the throng, and now *I'm* horrified.

What are *they* doing here? *Get them out!*

Their mother must finally work it out because she suddenly yanks them by the arms and drags them down the hallway, their expressions startled, their little brains traumatised.

Good one, Mum. Great work, woman! That shit can't be unseen.

I am furious at that. I am suddenly furious with everyone—the gawkers who can't seem to tear their eyes away, and Una and Roco who look about as useful as a condom at a convent. And that slimy stranger in the shiny vest who is now perched on the edge of Dad's desk, one hand spread out casually behind him, messing up all the papers, the other holding the phone to his ear, having a good ole chinwag to the emergency services department, like he's chewing the fat.

But most of all I am furious with Tessa, who keeps trying to straighten my hair down and readjust that stupid, gaudy tiara she insisted I don last night. If she didn't kill me, she's sure acting like a suspect.

The police arrive extraordinarily fast. It feels like a matter of minutes, but maybe I'm getting confused. Is time different when you're dead?

There are no paramedics. Tall, Dark and Handsome must have told them it was pointless, and I am glad of that. Two less people to be traumatised by the spectacle. Just because they've seen it all before doesn't make them immune, or at least that's what I've read.

Two uniformed officers quickly take over. Tessa has been dragged to her feet and away from my corpse, at a distance, where she should have been all along. She now stands huddled in Roco's arms, bloodied and wide-eyed, splattering me all over Roco's bare chest, and there's a delicious irony in that but we haven't got time to be clever, I need to keep reporting.

I see Una moping behind them, hand now at her mouth. I'm not sure she's said a word in ten minutes.

"I'm so sorry," I hear Tessa say. No, *think*. Her lips haven't moved. It's coming from inside her brain.

Well, what do you know? I can read minds! I like the sound of that.

Tessa continues, thinking, *I'm sorry this had to happen, Maisie, honey. I'm so, so sorry I didn't protect you.*

She's clearly talking to me, but what does she mean by that? Why did it *have* to happen and *whom* did I need protecting from?

What the hell have you been up to, Tessa? I think, for the second time tonight.

CHAPTER 5

After such a delayed discovery, I am startled by the rapid response. The two officers have morphed into four, no, make that six. One of them, a burly bloke with a buzz haircut, has corralled the guests into the living room and is now giving them a lecture. Something about providing statements, contact details, that kind of thing.

The young mum steps forward and barely says a word before she and her boys are ushered to the side and then very quickly out the door, past the pool and through the back garden gate. She can give her statement tomorrow, and thank goodness for that. Her kids should be tucked up safely in bed, not witnesses to a homicide. The youngest kid's four, maybe five. The oldest looks barely six and particularly stunned, like he's just seen a ghost. But really all he's seen is an empty carcass. He'd be more freaked out if he realised the ghost hovers above his head, scolding his mother for keeping him out so late.

As they take off, the other guests start giving their statements, and I try to listen in, but there's lots of hand wringing and head shaking and "sorry but I never heard a thing." I guess we can blame Justin Bieber for that.

I notice one uniformed officer interrogating Una and Jonas, who are providing my details rather than their own. He's scribbling it all down in a spiral notepad, his sticky-outy ears bobbing up and down as he writes. Jonas's hands are now fists at his side; Una's arms wrapped tight around her torso. Unlike many others, she's fully dressed, yet she looks colder than all of them. She's shivering beneath her cream linen jacket.

There are now four squad cars out the front, and another two officers, these ones in baggy blue overalls and chunky black boots, are hovering over me, swallowing back their smiles, like I've made their night. I'm almost expecting them to turn and high-five each other.

"Mickey's on the way," says the man, young, pretty, with wiry blond curls and thick blond eyelashes. He looks like he's just dropped off a wave and has left his board out the back.

"Thanks, Kelly," the woman says. She's shorter, stockier, and looks more suited to a footy field. She has an air of authority about her and is obviously the one in charge. Or at least I hope she is. I'd put money on her over the surfer dude any day.

"Pretty, wasn't she?" the woman says, casting her eyes from my face to the diamanté tiara and back, and I can almost feel myself blush.

"Looks high maintenance to me," comes the dude's response. Ouch.

The woman smirks. "Sorry, I forgot. You prefer them to sit quietly on the beach, holding your towel, right?"

He doesn't get a chance to respond. A uniformed officer is now standing at the study door. "Suspicious circumstances?" he asks.

It's the policeman with the Prince Charles ears, and Kelly snorts at him, then darts his eyes towards the gun and then back at the gaping hole in my head.

"What? I'm allowed to ask," comes the officer's sulky retort.

"You're *supposed* to ask," says the woman, shooting Kelly a frown. "That's your job, mate. Never make assumptions. Never take anything for granted. So, yes, I've declared this a crime scene; let's get on with it." She turns to look at him. "You're one of the first responders?"

He steps forward. "Yes, ma'am. Constable Craig DeWill from North Sydney Police St—"

She cuts him short. "You're with my team now. I want you reporting directly to me, got it?" His beam intensifies. "So, talk me through it; what have you learned?"

Big-eared Craig produces his notepad and clears his throat. "Right, so... the er, victim's name is Maisie May, aged twenty-seven. Currently resides at this address, which also happens to be her parents' house."

"Bit old for that, isn't she?" says Kelly. I'm hating him more by the second.

Craig ignores this. "Discovered about twenty minutes ago by a man named—" He refers to his notepad, looks lost for a moment, which earns him a snigger from Kelly. Finally he stabs at the page and says, "Jonas! Jonas Holder... no, *Hodder*. Aged thirty-one. Says he was on his way out."

"Out of the party?"

"That's what he said."

"So, what? He mistook the office for the driveway?"

Good point, I think, but Craig is shrugging like it's a moot point. "He appears to be quite intoxicated, ma'am, as do most of the witnesses. And I'm not just talking alcohol. The first responders located some cannabis in a bowl in the kitchen, and on the living room coffee table what appears to be MDM—"

"I really couldn't care less what party treats these people were into, Craig," the boss says.

She is still staring at me intensely, and I wish I could open my eyes and smile back at her. It's so good to see she has her priorities straight, although that's certainly not a word I'd use for my friends. They really *were* reenacting *The Hangover* tonight.

"The vic was pretty sloshed too, or so a few of the guests say. She was falling about a bit, slurring her words."

Goodness, how embarrassing. I know the cocktails were delicious, but I can't remember drinking *that* much.

25

"Any word on the parents?"

Craig clears his throat again. Is he nervous? Is this his first corpse, or is it the fact that he's just been recruited to the homicide squad that's making him rattle? He glances back at his trusty pad.

"David and Mandy May. Visiting relatives in Dubbo, I'm told, but the vic's best friends don't seem to have a working contact number for them. One of them's tried a few times, and there's no response. No one has any idea where they might be staying."

"Bugger," she says.

He nods. "There's two siblings, as well, two older brothers apparently."

"Apparently or is that a fact? Seems like a pretty easy one to substantiate."

He blanches, looks a little flummoxed again. "Er, yes, she definitely has two older brothers, but again, no one knows where they are or has a contact number for them either. One lives locally; one's out from the UK."

"Any of them here tonight?"

"Affirmative. One brother was here earlier apparent—" He catches himself. "He *was* at the party, but he must have left." He coughs, blushes. "He *did* leave. Sergeant Tanner—that's my boss, ma'am." He hesitates. "I mean, my normal boss. You probably need to talk to him about me working for—"

"Get on with it, Craig."

He clears his throat. "So, yes, Tanner has already had the premises searched, and there's no sign of the siblings. No next of kin anywhere, just friends."

The lead detective sighs heavily. "Dammit. Where is her family when you need them? Has anyone thought to check local hotels? Didn't you say one brother is visiting from overseas?"

"Yep, and the other one lives locally."

"So look him up. His details must be on file."

Craig grabs a pen from a pocket and makes a note.

"I'm onto it."

"Good. What else have you got?"

Another glance at the pad. "Right, so, the party's been going since about six this evening, give or take. Peaked around eleven and most of the guests cleared out by the time the vic was discovered—"

"Can we call her by her name, please?" The woman interrupts. "She was a person, yes? A human being?"

Kelly snorts, Craig blushes, and I become even fonder of the lead detective. I think she's a keeper.

"Sorry, ma'am. Yes, Ms May—"

"Maisie. Let's stick to that, shall we?" She glances down at me. "I reckon she'd be cool with us using her given name." Oh how I really wish I could smile.

"Of course, yes, um, so the party for *Maisie* was put on by some of her friends to 'cheer her up.' That's a direct quote."

"And why would Maisie need cheering up?" the boss asks just as an elegantly dressed woman steps into the house.

It's like a soap star has strayed onto the wrong set. With her flowing silk dress, undulating auburn locks, and a face so meticulously made up she could do a Revlon commercial, the woman doesn't look anything like a detective, but she earns the reverence of one, and I watch as she sweeps straight past the uniformed officers and down the hallway. She has a large black carryall in her hand and turquoise plastic gloves already in place. At least she got the props right. Must be the forensic pathologist I decide, watching as she slips off her kitten heels and pulls two matching plastic slippers over her feet before she enters the study. Oddly, the booties complete the look.

"Michaelia!" the boss says, helpfully. "Hello."

"Hey, Ruth, thanks for dragging me away. I didn't really want to finish that mascarpone trifle anyway."

The detective—Ruth, it seems—chuckles. "Sorry about that. Hot date?"

"Didn't even get past simmering stage. But the food was to die for." She doesn't stop to apologise for that woeful pun, just looks down at me through false eyelashes and says, "So what grief has come of this fair night?"

Ruth gives Craig the nod, and he begins repeating everything he's just said, so I take a moment to focus on the living room—or the living, to be precise.

Tessa is now being questioned by the officer with the buzz cut, and she still looks stunned and distraught. She can't be acting, surely? She never majored in Drama.

"I should have hung out with her more tonight. I could have been *with* her. I might have stopped…" She glances around the room, then holds a fist to her mouth.

Like she could stand between me and a killer with a loaded gun.

"And where exactly were you when your friend was shot?"

"In the pool," she says, talking through her fist as though hoping to muffle the truth. "I was in the *pool*, can you believe it? I was *swimming* and having *fun*. How could I *do* that to her? How could I let her *down*, how could I…"

And then she breaks into sobs again, her fleshy shoulders shaking so much it causes the towel to unravel as she falls back into Roco's arms. He glares at the officer like he wants to thump him.

"And you, sir?" the officer says. "Where were you when the shot rang out?"

"I… I didn't hear the shot. Did anyone?" He makes a show of looking around. "First I knew of this was when Jonas starting screaming like a baby."

"He'd just found poor Maisie!" Tessa gasps, shaking herself free of him and reaching for her towel.

I can't help but smile. Maybe my death will be the unmaking of them.

"I'm just saying," Roco continues, "if I had heard the shot, I would've tried to help, tried to save her."

"And what's your relationship to the deceased?" the cop asks, and Roco hesitates.

"We're just friends," he says stiffly, before turning his gaze back to Tessa.

I'm sorry, but *what*? *Just friends*? Is he for real?

He might have been playing tonsil hockey with my bestie, but we hadn't officially broken up. Or had we?

The way Tessa is struggling to meet his eyes now makes me wonder.

CHAPTER 6

Roco and I had a pretty solid relationship. Or at least I thought we had.

We met at a glittering charity event about eighteen months ago. I was there to raise awareness for some bleeding-heart cause. He was there to pick up, or so he liked to joke whenever anyone asked.

The truth is he's got a bigger heart than he cares to admit. If a mangy dog strayed across his path, he'd scoop it up and take it home before I even got a chance, and that was my forte, that was my domain.

I wonder now if I was the mangy dog. Is that why he took me in? Or was I the one doing the rescuing? It all feels so muddy now.

He is a bit like a meaty bulldog my Roco (or at least he *was* my Roco once). He's well under six foot, with a mop of dirty-brown hair and dark stubble on his beefy cheeks. I know he hits the gym and does weights, and I guess it keeps the fat at bay, but fully clothed he looks more Arnott's Biscuits than Arnold Schwarzenegger, and he'll have to keep up the exercise if he wants to avoid the fate of his forefathers (his dad's the size of a garden shed). There's a lot of Greek in him, I believe, and that includes regular helpings of his mother's mouthwatering moussaka.

There was a lot of love in him too. He ran a bubble bath fit for a queen, gave the best massage this side of

Kamalaya—complete with scented candles and classical music—and we never left the house without him checking I had my phone and my jacket. He would make a terrific dad, I think now, and now my heart flags.

It's only just occurred to me: I'll never get to be a mum. I'll never get to nag someone to remember to take their jacket…

Sorry.
Give me a moment.

Okay. I know you want to get back to my murder. I realise you're probably bored senseless with all this. But I wonder if it has any bearing. I wonder if it can shed some light. Did I stumble in on Roco and Tessa together? Did a fight ensue? Did things get out of hand, somehow out of control?

The police officer clearly doesn't think so because he's moved away from Roco and is now talking to Constable Craig. They are flipping through matching notepads and shaking their heads like something doesn't add up. Then the former calls the crowd to attention, clapping his hands loudly, and I soon realise what it is that's troubling them.

"Ladies and gentleman!" he yells out. "People! Attention please! This is very important. If anyone has any information regarding the May family and their whereabouts, I need you to step forward immediately. We need more information on the next of kin, particularly the two brothers."

They still haven't tracked down my family. I almost feel relieved. My folks are still snoring somewhere, blissfully ignorant of the hell that is about to unfold. It gives me some solace, although I know they'll have to wake up eventually.

"As for the rest of you"—the officer is still speaking—"we need to get all your details before the SOCOs get here, so please bear with us and we'll have you out of here as fast as we can."

"SOCOs?" someone asks. Tessa's pal Leslie, I think.

"Scenes of Crime Officers," whispers Tall, Dark and Handsome, like he's an expert.

"I can't believe they haven't found her parents yet," says Arabella, and there are sombre nods all round.

Tessa says, "I can't believe I don't know her brother's home address. Paul only lives about five minutes' drive away. To think she's lying there while he…"

She trails off, and Roco scoffs. "Cops are bloody useless. Why don't they just look him up? They have all our data on file now. Big Brother knows everything, so why can't they find him? I could do it for them in five seconds! *And* I told them where they could find the older brother Peter. What's taking them so long?"

Now there are universal shrugs, but Tessa is more interested in beating herself up.

"If only I could remember where the Mays stay when they visit the hospital. Can't be that many hotels in Dubbo surely?"

"Why don't they just call their mobile?" asks Roco.

Ha, ha, ha. I laugh at that one. We've been together for ages, and he still doesn't know my folks are Luddites? I did get them a spanking-new Samsung Galaxy once, but I'm pretty sure it's still sitting in its box in a kitchen drawer somewhere.

"If someone wants to chat, they'll call us on the landline," my mother always said.

"But what if they really need you and you're not home?" I asked.

"If we're not home, it means we're out and busy so we're not much use to them, are we?"

Can't argue with that logic.

I see Una pull out her own phone and check her messages. "I've called David's iPhone half a dozen times, left three messages, but it's obviously switched off."

Hang on, what's she on about? Is she referring to my *dad*, David? I didn't even realise he had an iPhone, let alone gave Una the number. It reminds me of something, but I can't think what.

A sudden snaky hiss catches my attention. It's coming from the sidelines again, from the crazy people near the light. It's quite horrific to think they're still there, watching me like stalkers.

"Go away!" I call out to them.

Why aren't they getting this? I look nothing like Whoopi Goldberg; they can pass on their own creepy messages.

"Come to the light!" one of them calls out, and I balk at that cliché.

Forget about it, folks. There's no way I'm crossing over yet. *Come on, Death, I need more time!* The party hasn't wrapped up, and my body's not even cold yet.

Back in the study, Michaelia is crouched down low on one side of me, using what looks like a cocktail swizzle stick to prod my gaping head while Ruth crouches near the gun, staring as if mesmerised. She looks up as Craig approaches.

"Any word yet on the next of kin?" Ruth asks.

He waggles a hand in the air. "We've been informed that the older brother is staying at the InterContinental, the one in Double Bay, but we still haven't been able to track him down."

"Not back in his room?"

"Not there at all according to the receptionist. Says he's a frequent visitor, but he didn't book in this trip. They haven't seen him there since last Christmas."

"Well that's bloody inconvenient. And the other brother?"

"We've located his home address, on Dulwich Road, just nearby, but there's no sign of life there."

"He's out? At this hour?"

"Not sure where he is, but there's a SOLD sign out the front of the house."

"What does that mean?"

He doesn't dare ponder a guess, and she looks even more irritated.

"Okay." She blows a puff of air through her lips. "Keep on it." Then she directs her gaze back to the weapon. "While you're questioning everyone, find out if any of them know anything about this firearm. I want to know who owns it. We can't make any assumptions yet. Oh and ask who has experience shooting. The shooter is an expert shot."

That's a brilliant idea! Most Australians wouldn't know how to fire a gun even if their life depended on it.

Kelly rolls his eyes for some reason—it's becoming *such* an annoying habit—while Craig returns to the living room (how apt is that name on a night like this?) and Ruth now stares at the hole in my head.

"It's amazing the damage a bullet can do," says Michaelia, reading her thoughts.

"Seen many?"

"Not enough. Hendo spent a month in LA a few years back. The wounds he saw, wow, amazing."

Amazing? You'd think they were discussing a trip to Space Mountain, but Ruth is nodding like she gets it.

"So, gun to the temple? Pop?" She makes a fake shooting motion with her fingers.

Michaelia nods. "Looks like it."

"Dare I ask?" Ruth says, and I get a creeping feeling.

Don't do it, I think. *Don't go there, Ruth.*

And then she does.

She says the thing I know you've all been considering. "Suicide?"

The word hangs in the air like a disgusting stench.

CHAPTER 7

Before Michaelia gets a chance to answer, Ruth redeems herself and adds, "Or could it be murder?"

The pathologist stares down at me as if weighing it up while I feel a flash of red-hot anger.

Oh give me a break!

I know it's been the elephant in the room since this whole saga began, but it isn't suicide, folks, I can assure you of that. I wouldn't do that to myself. More importantly, I wouldn't do it to my parents. I might have been in a low patch, but I wouldn't take my own life, knowing how cruelly that would ruin the lives of everyone else. That's not the kind of person I am. Or at least the kind of person I *was*. Now... well, now...

Thankfully Michaelia's not so quick to judge.

"Wish it was that open and shut," she says. "The proximity of the weapon certainly works, but it could be a setup. I've seen a few of those." She takes my hand into her gloved fingers, and it feels like a touching gesture until I realise what she's up to. "I'll check for gunshot residue and call the blood splatter specialist in, but we may not know for sure for some time."

Ruth nods. "Can you at least give me a time of death?"

Now Michaelia raises one thickly pencilled eyebrow. "Well, I'm not here for my gorgeous looks."

I think Kelly might beg to differ. He's gone suspiciously quiet since she arrived and has been watching her work a little too intensely. Either he's considering a career change, or he's got a major crush.

Mickey continues. "She's been dead at least an hour, I'd say, maybe an hour and a half, max."

Really? Time sure flies when your friends are having fun.

"You sure?" This is Craig, and it earns him another raised eyebrow from Mickey. I'm learning it's her trademark—the raised eyebrow, a slight tilt of those luscious curls. One that says "You dare to question me, you vermin?"

"Sorry," he says quickly, "it's just that we only got the call through about forty minutes ago. So what were they all doing for the forty or so minutes before that?"

"That's for them to know and you to find out," she replies, her eyebrow dropping as she waves someone over.

It's a tattooed woman in a blue jumpsuit who's been hovering by the doorway. She has a digital camera in her inked hands.

"Get both angles of the head and the hands, thanks, JJ," Mickey says.

"And I want the position of that gun before I bag it," adds Ruth, who then turns to Craig. "When exactly was this called in?"

He checks his notes. "Twelve seventeen p.m."

"Caller still here?"

"I believe, er, *yes*. Yes he is."

"Get him in here now."

Mr Tall, Dark and Handsome strides into the room, the confidence of a police commissioner in his swagger. It seems odd that he's such a key player in all this, considering I only just met him tonight. He doesn't seem to find it odd at all. It feels like he's done all this before, or maybe he's been preparing for this instead. How's that for a sinister deduction?

"I'm Detective Sergeant Ruth Powell. I'm in charge of

this investigation," she begins. "Thanks for your time, Mr…?"

"Vijay Singh," he says, politely filling the space. "*Doctor* Vijay Singh."

We're both looking at him sideways now. Ruth says, "Have we met before? You look familiar."

Something flickers behind those dark eyes of his. It's the first crinkle in his otherwise smooth demeanour, but he recovers quickly and shakes his topknot. "I don't believe so, no."

She nods slowly, eyes squinting. She's making a mental note to look him up.

"You're a GP?"

"A doctor of philosophy."

Her eyes relax again; she looks suitably unimpressed. She is thinking, *Doctor of bad hairstyles more like.* And I am thinking she's hilarious. (I don't know *why* I can hear some thoughts and not others, but I'm grateful I can hear Ruth's. It's like she's keeping me in the loop.)

Ruth asks about his phone call, and he tells her what we already know. Hottie started screaming, everybody came running, he called the cops.

"And you dialled triple zero immediately?"

"Give or take a minute. There was some discussion about calling an ambulance, but I knew that was unnecessary. She was clearly deceased."

Ruth's eyes squint again. "We believe she may have been *deceased* as long as forty minutes before she was discovered. Any idea why no one heard the gunshot?"

He shrugs like it's obvious. "It was a party. Insanely loud music, lots of laughter. Usual stuff."

"Okay, how about the body then. The office is not that far from the front door. It's just near the inside guest bathroom. How could no one have spotted her on their way in or out?"

"Good question, Detective Powell. You've got me there." He checks his hair, as though worried the topknot might have taken off. "Except, well, I do believe the door was originally closed, although you'd have to confirm that with the first witness. Jonah, I think his name was. Something like that. And the party had primarily moved to the pool by then anyway. I can only assume that most people used the facilities out the back. There's a small loo to the side of the pergola. There's also a gate out onto the laneway from the back garden. A better way to exit if you don't want to drip through the house."

She nods casually, but I'm looking at him twice again. He seems creepily familiar with the property layout, don't you think? I have a hunch he's been here before. I have a hunch he's not who he says he is.

Perhaps it's time we take a closer look at Mr Tall, Dark and Handsome, Vijay Singh.

At a party with almost one hundred guests at its peak, many of them friends of friends, some clearly gatecrashers, it's only natural I didn't know all of them, including Mr Tall, Dark and Handsome. (Do you mind if I keep using the moniker? I think it suits him better.) But there was something suspicious about him from the start.

I'm not even sure we were properly introduced. I do know he was by Una's side for the first half of the night, and so I assumed they were together. As you do when you see people clinging to each other like soggy lettuce. Yet he kept sneaking glances at me, over his wineglass, his dark lashes batting lazily, a coy smile on his lips.

He was incredibly flirtatious.

I let him have a good long look at one point, hoping that would satiate his curiosity and put him off. I mean, I can bat eyelashes with the best of them, but I'm not into stealing other people's men.

I'm not Tessa McGee, for instance.

So, Mr Tall, Dark and Handsome—sorry, *Doctor* Tall, Dark and Handsome—a man that everybody else seemed to know except me, approached at one point and asked how I was.

I said, "I'm fine, thank you. How's Una?"

He smiled as if I was an amusing imbecile. "We're not together. Is that what you think?"

Then he took my hand into his own and started inspecting my palm like he was about to read my future as he said, "I was wondering if you want to go somewhere more private, maybe upstairs?"

Urgh. Yuck! I snatched my hand back.

"Don't be like that," he said.

And I said, "Like what?" before turning away and smashing straight into Una's breasts.

She's super tall, did I tell you that? Well over six foot, with legs up to her ears a la Darryl Hannah from that movie *Splash*.

"What's going on?" she said, glancing from Tall, Dark and Handsome, then down to me and back.

"Nothing," I replied, blushing despite myself.

Her eyes narrowed, and she stared hard at the Lothario behind me, but I wasn't hanging around to deal with the fallout. I excused myself and scurried off towards the kitchen. I don't know what happened next. I don't know if she eventually tracked me down and we had a fight and she killed me in the heat of the moment, but I can't see that playing out.

If Una shot me for "flirting" with her new beau, she'd have to be shockingly insecure, and that's not a trait that sits easily with Una. She's the kind of woman who can give a rousing speech at a moment's notice, who eats meals at busy restaurants on her own *without a book*, and even goes on exotic holidays *todo solo*. She's just back from three days in Bangkok and never even thought to drag someone along. I would have gone, if only she'd asked me and if only I had the cash.

Una's one of the most confident women I know, as you would be when you have the looks of Daryl Hannah and the smarts of a lawyer—did I mention she's a lawyer, an actual real lawyer, not a lowly PA? What's not to be confident about?

Yet, despite that, she rarely has a boyfriend, and I have a feeling I know why. She has dangerous taste in men. They're never suitable; it always self-destructs. I have a theory about Una, but I won't bore you with it now. Let's just say she has commitment issues and leave it at that.

Anyway, moving right along, while we're on the subject of suspects, shall we tick another one off? Let's take another look at Tessa. My nemesis.

We're actually best friends if I'm being honest, but it doesn't mean she didn't bring me down from time to time. We've been besties for twenty-four years, ever since she popped her head around the paint easel at kindergarten to say "Hawo" or some such thing.

"Oh, darling, you were hiding behind there and shaking like a leaf!" My mother loves to remind everyone whenever she gets the chance. "And lovely Tessa took you by your chubby little hand and dragged you out."

Tessa always smiles smugly at this retelling, as though I would be cowering there still if she hadn't stumbled over and rescued me.

Suffice to say, we became "thick as thieves" after that—my mother's words, not mine. I love Tessa, I really do, but sometimes I wonder whether she's one of those friends you stay friends with for no real reason other than a shared history, a common neighbourhood and a lot of habit. She lives a few doors down, across the street. We just fell in with each other and forgot to fall out.

Until tonight.

Yep, that's when everything clicked. She is having an affair with Roco. I just know it. I didn't need to spot them snogging or groping or anything that crass. It was suddenly very obvious. The way they held themselves. The way they avoided each other's eyes. The way the air sparked like faulty Christmas lights whenever they got close. Roco never sparked like that for me.

"What are you *doing?*" I said to Tessa about halfway through the night.

She stared at me blankly. "What?"

I stared back. And then she blushed. Quite literally, she turned a beetroot shade of red. And I thought, *Hook, line and sinker.*

"Really, Tessa? *Really?*" I said and then shook my head and walked away. Because I didn't really want to face the facts. I didn't want to hear her say "Yes, we're at it like rabbits" or "Sorry, but we're soul mates, we just can't help ourselves" or whatever inane justification was bubbling away in her big fat head.

So I stumbled off to the kitchen where I found Tall, Dark and Handsome deep in conversation with another woman, the aforementioned Arabella. I wondered if he'd tried to read her palm and if she'd fallen for that trick.

They both swept around to stare at me as I walked in, and the look of guilt in Arabella's eyes was all the answer I required.

I wondered if Una knew just how sleazy her new boyfriend was. I was planning to find her and ask. I was hoping we could lick our wounds together, but Una was nowhere to be found. Until I did find her, ten minutes later, rummaging about in my dad's study, leafing through the contents on his desk.

What was she doing in there?

"What are you doing in here?" I asked as she swept up and around to look at me. If there was an innocent explanation, her spontaneous babble belied it.

"What? Me? Huh? No!"

A bizarre splutter of words if ever I heard some. She'd lost her usual confidence.

"What are you looking for?" I asked.

"Nothing! No, nothing at all!"

Then she backed away slowly from the desk as though it contained live explosives and sprinted out the door, and

I was left to peer at the papers on top to try to comprehend. Apart from some bank slips and unopened junk mail, I spotted light pink stationery, a Qantas boarding pass and a wad of cash, which made me think twice.

My folks wouldn't leave a fistful of hundred-dollar notes lying about. Did Una just put them there? And if so, *why*?

I never got a chance to explore that further because Roco suddenly appeared and dragged me by the hand and led me back to the party—it was cake time! Hurrah! Let's cut the stupid sponge cake! Even though it wasn't my birthday and I didn't want a cake, especially not a mushy strawberry sponge one with fake cream filling.

I was going to go back to the study. I was going to store that cash somewhere safe, but someone must have beat me to it because I'm staring at Dad's desk *right now* and I can tell you, there's not so much as a dollar in sight.

And now that I think about it, the pink stationery has also gone walkabout.

CHAPTER 8

Before I can give that any more thought—and it is super interesting, don't you think?—Buzz Cut claps his hands and makes another announcement. What is it with him and grand announcements? He doesn't even have much to impart. Just asks the throng to hurry up and finish giving their statements and bugger off, although he says it slightly more diplomatically than that.

"And be sure to use the exit out by the pool," he adds. "Nobody is to step through the living room door and back into the house. We have officially secured the scene."

I'm not going anywhere, I hear Tessa think. *I'm not leaving poor Maisie alone with you lot.*

And suddenly I don't care if she's sleeping with my boyfriend or not. I want to reach down and hug her tight.

Una, meanwhile, is in a corner madly tapping away on her mobile phone. I try to zoom in. I try to see what's on the screen, but like the computer in Dad's office, it's just a bunch of hieroglyphics. Is she messaging my folks? Is that it? I can't even read her thoughts to find out. I try, very hard, but her mind is like a closed book.

Come on, Death! Throw me a bone!

Why can't I see what Una's doing? What's that about? I'm also intrigued by this mind-reading business. If I can read minds, and clearly I can—Leslie's wondering if Hottie Hodder is still single, Arabella is wondering where she misplaced an earring and Mattie has "Despacito" on a loop in his head—why can't I read Una's mind or, more importantly—and let's just hope they're mutually exclusive—the mind of my *killer*? Why can't I hear someone chuckle to themselves while thinking *Mwahahaha. I got away with murder!*

It's a fair question, don't you think?

And I have so many more where that came from, like how come I can suddenly see straight into all the bathrooms as well as the guest bedroom, which contains nothing more incriminating than a ruffled bed cover? I don't know exactly why that particular room was previously blacked out, but I have a feeling it has something to do with a scantily clad Arabella and her missing earring.

Who was she in there with, I wonder, and why were they hiding that from me?

"Pssst!"

That's the drooling woman near the light again. Louder, more insistent. She's just not giving up. I stare at her. I sigh. She looks like she's been back there a while. I guess she may have some answers for me. Shall we indulge her? Just for a bit?

I glance back at the house. My friends are slowly being ticked off by the police (in every sense of the word, for Roco at least) and shuffled on their way, the detectives still inspecting my corpse, other officers now ransacking the house. Big Ears is in Mum's sewing room and staring at the makeshift bed in the corner like it's out of place. And I guess it is. Mum must have set it up for Peter, hoping he'd stay over. For once.

There's not much to report, so I give up on the living. I swallow my nerves and I head towards the light.

We've all heard about the infamous pearly gates and the long, dark tunnel that leads to the "afterlife," but from this angle all I can see is a dingy archway, three seriously deformed dead people and not a pearl in sight.

The oldest, the woman who'd been waving like the Queen Mum, drifts forward as I approach and offers me a sympathetic smile.

"Hello, Maisie," she says, her voice low and slow, oozing concern. "How are you *feeling*, darling? Are you *okay*?"

I snort at her. "You're about an hour and forty minutes too late."

She nods, her smile sadder. "A little longer than that, I'd say."

Humph! Like she can talk. "The question is, are *you* okay?" I snap back.

I can see the haunted look in her eyes. I can see the dribble running down her face. She knows it's there, right?

The woman wipes one cheek self-consciously. "I'm just here to help you across."

"Were you the victim of a vicious murder too?" I ask.

Now her smile deflates. Pain crosses the threshold of her face. "I guess you could say that," she says, then sniffing, adds, "Two murders in fact."

Before I can digest that bizarre comment, the young man behind her calls out in a singsong voice.

"*Helloooo*? What am I? Chopped liver?"

His face is black-and-blue, his body broken, one arm dangling oddly from its socket, his right hand a mash of bone and pulpy flesh. He does look a little like chopped liver, but I'm too polite to say so.

I hear a tiny snigger and spot a teenage girl hovering behind him. She's probably sixteen but looks about twelve, as thin as a twig, deep hollows under her eyes, a beanie on her head.

Blimey, it's like a floating horror show back here.

"No offence, guys, but you're not the most comforting welcoming committee."

The man looks completely mortified by this comment. He attempts to straighten his dangling arm, but the older woman places a hand softly on his shoulder and says,

"Ignore her. She's just angry."

"I think she's still at denial, actually." He gives me the once-over. "Just because you're dazed and confused, honey, doesn't mean you gotta take it out on the rest of us."

"Hey, it's not my job to communicate with the living."

He stares at me, bemused. "What are you on about?"

"Haven't you got some creepy message you want me to pass on to your bestie or something?"

"Huh?"

"We're just here to help you across," the middle-aged woman explains, and now I'm really cranky.

"Well, I'm sorry I've wasted your time, but I didn't ask you to come and drag me to the light. I'm quite happy where I am, thanks very much."

"Sure you are," says the man, rolling his bloodshot eyes. "That bullet wound looks like a barrel of laughs."

"Ouch!" I say, reaching for my head and patting some of my hair down across the gaping hole. I realise the tiara is still there, clinging on, and I reposition that while I'm at it.

They all watch me with varying degrees of pity.

"Let's start over, shall we?" says the woman, her tone upbeat. "I'm Deseree. This is Neal, and behind him young Emie. It's Neal's first official chaperone job."

"Really? And here I was thinking he was an old hand." I flick my eyes to his smashed limb and grin.

Neal looks fit to burst, but Deseree has him by the shoulder again. "Maybe just let me take this one for now."

Neal sneers but drifts back, muttering something about practise and how he'll never get his points up, like he's discussing frequent-flier miles and I'm standing between him and a free trip to Bali. Then he attempts to fold his arms across his chest, nightclub bouncer-style, but the dislocated arm flops back down again. I try not to laugh.

Deseree draws me away from them just a little. "So, Maisie, do you understand what's happened to you?"

I shrug. "It's pretty open and shut. I've clearly been shot in the head by person or persons unknown."

I can hear both Neal and Emie sniggering now. They think I deserved it.

"You really don't know who did this to you? You didn't see?" Deseree asks.

"No! Honest. I've forgotten the whole event. Why, is that important?"

"It is if you want to cross, my darling, yes. You need to work it out."

"Why don't we just put her out of her misery and tell her whodunit?" calls Neal.

Deseree shoots him a stern look. "Because that's against the rules and you know that very well, Neal. Thou shall see when—"

"Thoust is ready to see, yeah, yeah," he says.

"Huh?"

A sheet of paper has materialised in Deseree's hands, and she holds it out to me.

"The Rules of Death," she says. "They're quite inflexible. But they'll make total sense at the end, I promise you that. It's important you come to terms with what's happened to you and why it happened, otherwise your spirit will be in limbo and you'll never settle in."

"Well, we wouldn't want to be unsettled now, would we?" I say sarcastically, snatching the sheet from her. "Nothing remotely unsettling about any of this."

I stare at the sheet in my hand. It's not actually a sheet, at least not one made of paper. It's like a floating iPad screen, as thin as a strand of cotton and just as flexible. It's lit from within, words sketched across the front in an old English font. Black Chancery by the look of it. I wonder if Steve Jobs has had a hand in the design. He's back there somewhere, right?

I glance down and begin to read.

C.A. LARMER

The Rules of Death
© *Forever*

*1. Thou shalt not hear what the living do not
wish thee to hear.*

*2. Thou shalt not see what the living do not
wish thee to see.*

*3. Thou shalt not invade the living's thoughts
unless invited in.*

4. Thou shall see all when thou is open to seeing.

*5. Thou shall make thy way towards the light
at the earliest opportunity.*

*6. Once registered at Forever, thou shalt not return
beyond the light without express permission.*

*7. Thou shall be granted one final wish
upon entering the light.*

I only get as far as the second rule before I'm frowning back at her.

"Well that's a load of nonsense because I can tell you this much: I keep seeing things that I'm pretty sure the living don't want me to see."

"Such as?"

"Such as my best mate flirting with my boyfriend."

"Maybe they *do* want you to see that," says Emie, her voice barely a whisper, but it smashes across me like a roaring wave. I flinch.

Why would they do that to me?

"Probably enjoy hurting you," says Neal, who has clearly just read my thoughts. He smiles when he hears me think that, and so I take the opportunity to think, *You are a total dickhead.*

48

Takes one to know one, he thinks back.

"Now, now, children," says Deseree, who's also a mind reader, "let's keep it civil, and this will all be over before you know it."

"I don't *want* it to be over!" I wail, knowing I sound like a toddler and wondering whether to stamp one foot for good measure. "I *need* to spend more time with my friends! I never got to finish my party! I never even got any *birthday cake*!"

"But it's not your birthday, and you don't even like sponge cake," hisses emaciated Emie, who looks like she could benefit from a very large slice.

She gasps at that thought, and I try to shake myself out of it. I try very hard to calm down.

"I'm sorry. I know I'm being a brat." I look at her properly and realise that she's also clearly a victim, but unless she's been lingering since the Holocaust, the poor thing, my guess is she had cancer. Probably leukaemia. She's the spitting image of a kid down the street who died of it a few years back.

"I'm sorry," I say again. "But give me a break, okay? I'm new at this. I'm still trying to come to terms with the idea of being dead, let alone murdered, and it really doesn't help if I can read some people's thoughts and not other's."

"Rules are rules," sings Neal.

"Well they're stupid rules then," I snap back. I soften my tone. I turn to Deseree. She seems amenable. "Please give me a little longer. I do want to solve my murder, but it's not that straightforward. For some reason I can't remember all the important bits, and it feels like everyone is hiding something from me; no one's being completely honest. If you could just let me hear what they're all thinking, then I'd have this sewn up in a flash."

Deseree is shaking her head. "It doesn't work like that."

"But *why*?"

She nods to the others, and they start to float back

inside the tunnel.

"Read the rules again, Maisie, read them properly this time."

I watch as the darkness swallows her whole, and then I openly scowl. Thanks for nothing, weirdos. Thanks for all your help.

I take a deep breath and float back to Mother Earth where I notice that Detective Sergeant Powell is making her way up the interior staircase towards my bedroom. I can see Kelly's already up there, poking through my belongings, a pitiful expression on his face. What he's looking for I cannot say, but I doubt he'll find much. I may have redecorated and moved back a few months ago, but I never really moved back in. If you look closely, you can see half my stuff is still in my suitcase, several cardboard boxes of crap still sitting there unopened.

"I'll pop these away then, shall I?" I remember Mum saying, and I remember screaming at her that I could do it myself and to leave me alone and to get the hell out.

I had to trudge downstairs to find her and apologise for that.

"I know it's a difficult time," she said stiffly, stopping short at the "but."

I pulled her into a hug. "I'll be better, Mum, I promise. I just need to sort my head out. I'll be okay."

The sad smile she gave me told me what she thought of that.

Was I really such a screwup?

And if so, where did it all go wrong? I had a thriving career once, I had a boyfriend, I had a sharehouse in the city and friends who didn't cheat on me. So what the hell happened?

I hear a cup smash, but it's another flashback.

I hear the smash long before I register what it is I have done. It's my favourite work cup, the one that says MY WAY OR THE HIGHWAY. The one I keep on my desk so the others won't use it and leave it smudged. It's in a dozen pieces on the floor of the kitchen at work, hot tea splattered everywhere, several sets of eyes watching me aghast. I did that. I smashed it.

When did I become so angry? So out of control? Such a brat? And, more importantly, why?

Detective Ruth is resting against the banister, staring into my bedroom.

"Anything?" she says to Kelly.

He looks up and shrugs. "Just a diary with lots of bleak poems, but she's no Dylan Thomas I can tell you that."

Ruth snorts. "And what would you know about Dylan Thomas, mate?"

"I know my poetry. I'm more than a pretty face, you know."

She snorts again. "Nothing about taking her own life?"

"Not a word."

I told you so.

"So what's with the meds then?"

She sounds like she's answering me back, and I follow her gaze to my bedside table where, sure, there are some antidepressants, I'll give her that. But don't you go and get excited either. If you all look closely, I think you'll find the box remains unopened. I just took the damn pills to humour Dr Marlin. He's the family GP.

Mum dragged me to see him after the Jonas incident, the one that's really not worth repeating. At least I don't think it is.

"These might help," Dr Marlin said, and my mother nodded vigorously, thinking that would sort me out, that and plenty of hugs and old-fashioned home cooking.

I guess I never got the chance to find out.

As I watch Ruth inspect the packet and then place them in an evidence bag, I wonder if I should have opened them. Maybe they would have been more useful than hugs and home cooking, not to mention that silly feathered contraption that flutters over Kelly's head, mocking me and any dreams I dared to have.

CHAPTER 9

Downstairs most of the guests have now cleared out, as instructed, and there's just a handful of my closest friends still loitering by the back gate, just on the other side of my house. (If you get lost, just ask Tall, Dark and Handsome, he seems to know his way about.)

I know what Tessa promised, but she may as well head off. My body has left the building; it took off in my absence. Mickey has vanished too, so I guess she escorted it out, although she could be back with her hot date for all I know, hooking into some leftover trifle. As I told you before, I can't see beyond Ivey Street (that's my street, in case you're wondering).

I *can* see inside some neighbouring houses, however, although not all, and can only assume from those ridiculous rules that those people have invited me in. Yet why old Mrs Russo would want me to see her standing in her floral nightie, peeking through the kitchen curtains like a paparazzo, I don't know.

"Go back to bed, Mrs Russo! Nothing to see here!"

Except that's not quite true.

There are still plenty of uniformed officers about, some now trampling through Mum's garden at the front of the house, others going door to door, interrogating the inhabitants who lean against doorways, clutching dressing gowns, eyes wide with voyeuristic delight. And who can blame them all? It is rather fascinating, in a ghoulish kind of way. This is my first murder too, and I'd be just as fascinated. In fact, the old me would be handing out pipes and trying to work out *whodunit*. If only I could channel the old me, the one who didn't smash cups and wasn't prescribed antidepressants.

I watch as a new team of characters start pulling up. Ah, it must be the *soccer* team, or *socco* or whatever Buzz Cut called them, judging by the white vans and the matching turquoise pullovers and the looks of bland proficiency about them. They don't seem anywhere near as enthusiastic as Ruth and Kelly, so I'm guessing they've been there, done that, bought the T-shirt…

You get the gist.

I'm happy the experts are here, to be honest. It's proof they're taking my murder seriously, and who knows, maybe they can shine some light on this dark and woeful night. Speaking of dark, I was about to follow them inside, but something in the gloomily lit laneway has caught my eye.

Someone is standing on the very edge of the thin lane that leads to that back gate, looking furtive. He has his hands wedged into his trouser pockets and is peering down towards my friends as though trying to catch someone's eye. Una's, I think, judging by the angle. But Una is not looking his way; she is talking in hushed tones to Leslie, but I can hear them loud and clear. They are remembering the last time they went clubbing with me. A long time ago by the sounds of it, and isn't that a pity and wasn't I the world's *worst* dancer. Ever.

"Like two ferrets trying to get out of a hessian bag," says Una, and they almost fall over with laughter.

Wow, thanks for that, ladies. Hope that gets a mention in the eulogy.

I glance back at the watching man and am not surprised to find that it is Vijay. Mr Tall, Dark and Handsome. He looks a little frustrated. He pulls his hands out of his pockets and brings one to his lips. It looks like he's about to whistle when something makes him stop, and he shoves his hands back into his pants. A police officer with large buttocks and a thin ponytail has rounded the end of the laneway and is calling out to him to get a move on.

"I'm on my way, Officer!" Tall, Dark and Handsome calls back, giving Una one more glance before turning away. Belatedly she spots him and raises her eyebrows, but it's too late. She has no clue what he wants, but I do.

Bad luck, bucko, you weren't quite furtive enough. I saw what you shoved in your pocket then. I know what that is.

It's a light pink envelope, just like the one I saw on Dad's desk earlier tonight. It looked a little pregnant, though, like it was "with letter."

Now we know who pilfered the stationery. The question, of course, is why?

Okay, how are you doing? Are you keeping up? Because, yes, it is a little curious that a virtual stranger would steal a letter from my father's study and then try to flag Una down with it. Is there something in the letter he wants to show her? Was he giving it to her? Or was he giving it *back*?

He certainly looked suspicious—the way he concealed it the moment the officer called out—and Una looked equally suspicious when I caught her hovering near that envelope earlier tonight. I thought she'd just deposited the cash. Now I wonder if that money was like the proverbial red herring, distracting me from what was really going on. Was Una dropping a letter off for my folks? Or was she leaving it there for Tall, Dark and Handsome to discover?

Are you as baffled right now as I am? We need to see what's in that envelope, that bit is clear. We need to read that letter, assuming it is a letter, and well, what else would you put inside a mushy-coloured envelope? I stare hard at Tall, Dark and Handsome's trousers (yes, bear with me, we have no choice). His pockets are camouflaged in the dark. I can't believe I'm saying this, but if only I had superpowers, I could see through pleated cotton.

Tall, Dark and Handsome is now striding down the street, heading towards a red sports car (what else would he drive?), and Una is now chatting with Arabella, but this time I can't hear a word they are saying. And, frankly, I'm relieved. If that last conversation is any indication, they've probably moved on to my karaoke skills ("like two cats screeching in the night").

A shrill mobile phone ring cuts through my thoughts, and I am forced away from my friends and back to the centre of the action, which has now moved from my bedroom to the kitchen, evidence bags piled up on the round pine table that sits in the very centre of the room. It's the place we usually eat our Corn Flakes.

The kitchen has become a makeshift headquarters, by the look of it, and Ruth is now standing at the open doorway, surveying the action. (Kelly is still in my room, by the way, one hand holding a phone to his ear, the other poking about. It makes me feel a little violated, if I'm honest, and I wish he'd do it with some more enthusiasm.)

I watch as a young woman with a black bob furiously clicks away on a laptop at the table, Buzz Cut standing over her, notepad in one hand. Craig is leaning against the oven door, talking to someone on his own phone while Ruth darts glances between all three of them.

She's waiting for something, but I can't tell what.

Eventually she says, "Okay, guys, settle down, let's see where we're at." She waits as Craig finishes his call, then she continues. "We still have far too many loose ends. We need to clear some up if we're ever gonna get some sleep tonight. Craig, tell me that was good news."

He gives her a so-so motion. "Dubbo Area Command is getting back to me."

"Dammit. What's the holdup?"

"It *is* two in the morning," he says gently.

"So what? They get to sleep and we don't?"

"I'm just saying."

"Just keep on it, okay?" She runs a hand through her hair. Stares at Buzz Cut. "Tanner, how did your people go? Find any evidence of a break-in? Tampering with the office door? Anything remotely unusual or suspicious?"

"Nope, sorry," he says, sounding anything but apologetic. "No one saw a thing, and we can't find anything interesting to report. Plenty of empty booze bottles, some joints, a couple of used condoms and some vomit out in the front garden—just your typical party paraphernalia. Well, apart for the stiff in the library, of course."

Ruth flinches at that, which is nice of her, but she doesn't pull him up on it, just congratulates herself for recruiting Craig to her team instead of this "buffoon."

"What about the brothers?" she persists. "Have we at least found one of the brothers yet?" The buffoon shrugs, so she turns to Black Bob. "Louise?"

The woman at the laptop shakes her head from side to side, her eyes never leaving the screen as her hair slaps across each cheek.

"Hey, guys, I just spoke to the Day Street police," Kelly says, pocketing his iPhone as he strides into the kitchen. "They've checked at hotels neighbouring the InterContinental and several of the better ones in the city, and the vic's brother Peter May hasn't booked into any of them." Under her glare he quickly adds, "I've also located a mobile number for him, but it appears switched off."

"Oh for goodness' sake. It's like the entire family has gone into hiding."

Ruth sighs and I sigh along with her.

I was happy they were sleeping peacefully, really I was, but now I think it's time for them to wake the hell up!

Ruth reaches for one of the evidence bags. "Right, first things first. We need to get this firearm down to forensics and get some fingerprints off it. Mickey is checking gun residue on Maisie's fingers as we speak."

Ah, good. She's got her priorities straight, and the trifle has come out second best.

"We should've tested everyone at the party, made them all give us their DNA," Tanner says, taking the bag from her, and Ruth shoots him a frown.

She's thinking it's high time he pissed off back to his cave. "That's not how we do things, mate. We find our suspect first, then we look for DNA. Better use of resources. And it's kind of polite not to treat everyone like a suspect."

He shrugs again.

"So you think there is a suspect, boss?" says Kelly. "It's not just suicide?"

"*Just* suicide?"

"You know what I mean." He saw the antidepressants. He thinks it's open and shut.

"I don't know anything at this stage and neither do you. The victim was found with a fatal head wound that could have been self-inflicted, granted, but we don't know that for a fact. Until Mickey comes back with a bit more substantiating evidence, we keep an open mind, and until I talk to the parents about their daughter's state of mind, I'm not making any assumptions."

"Her friends *did* say—"

"I know what her friends *said*, Tanner." She interrupts. "But maybe it's in the interests of those *friends* to say what they said. Ever think about that? You can't believe every single thing you're told in this business, right? We need to hear it from several sources before it becomes 'fact.'" She makes air quotes with her fingers, then drops them to the marble bench top and starts tapping away. "I *really* need to speak to the family."

And then, as if on cue, one of them starts screaming like Stanley Kowalski from the front of the house.

CHAPTER 10

"Peter!" comes a loud cry. Then more dramatically, "*Peeeeeeter!*"

Goodness, it really does sound like something out of a Tennessee Williams play, raw and heart-breaking, except that's my brother Paul down there bellowing his lungs out while a uniformed officer attempts to restrain him. It's the ponytailed woman who told Vijay to clear out.

Glad you could make the party, Paul, I think, but why are you screaming for Peter when I'm the one with the bullet in my head? Peter isn't even here; we've already established that. Well, neither am I, now that I think about it, but he doesn't know that.

"It's my *home*!" Paul cries to Door Bitch out the front. "It's my sister! I'm going in!"

"Your sister's body has now been removed, sir," the copper says calmly, one hand still on his chest, but it has the opposite effect.

"What? No! I didn't get to see her! I didn't get to say goodbye!"

"I'm sorry, sir. I can give you details for the morgue."

"*Morgue?*" He looks at her horrified.

Ruth appears then, Kelly close behind. "What's going on?" she calls out.

Ponytail goes to speak, but Paul pushes past her and up the remaining driveway to the front door.

"I'm Paul May," he cries out. "This is my parents'

59

house. I heard that my sister… she's…" Then his face crumples and he looks ready to drop.

Kelly rushes forward and grabs him under one shoulder while Ruth wraps a protective arm around the other, and together they shepherd him through the door and into the hallway, Ruth shooting a ferocious scowl at the officer at the front as she does so. *Moron,* that look says. *Idiot, imbecile.*

It's official. I'm in love.

"I am so sorry about that," she says gently, directing Paul towards the living room before realising the SOCOs haven't cleared that space yet. She steers him into the kitchen where she nods at Louise, who's still tapping away. The woman scoops her laptop up with one hand and, still tapping, scuttles out. Tanner and Craig have already vanished. Paul drops into the chair Louise just vacated, then places his elbows on the tabletop and his head into his hands.

Ruth gives him a moment, fetching him a glass of water, then flashes a final scowl in the general direction of the officer outside before saying, "I'm so sorry for your loss, Mr May. We've been trying to contact you and your family for the past two hours."

He looks up. Frowns.

"Isn't Peter here? Didn't he…" He lets that sentence dangle.

She waits a beat, then says, "Your brother left the party sometime ago, before your sister was discovered. We haven't been able to reach him either."

"What? *Really?*"

"Do you know where he might be? Have a contact number? We've tried him at the InterContinental, but we're told he hasn't booked in yet."

Paul looks confused by this before he starts to vigorously nod. "Yes, no, um, he's… he's staying at the Comfort Inn this time. The one just down the road."

Really? Peter's standards are dropping. Paul has other

thoughts. He's thinking, *He's been through every chambermaid in the city, has to start afresh on a new lot.*

He doesn't say that, thankfully, just adds, "Wanted to be closer to home."

And the wrinkle that suddenly appears between his eyebrows reveals what he thinks of that. He shakes himself a little and pulls out his mobile phone.

"I've got his number here somewhere." He begins scrolling through his device, finds it and then looks up at Ruth, who is still hovering over him protectively. "Should I…?"

"It's best we deliver the news in person, sir. Face-to-face." She calls Kelly over, who checks the number on Paul's screen and nods.

"That's the number I've got. It's not picking up."

Paul looks even more startled by this and starts plucking at his lower lip as though trying to draw blood.

Ruth tells Kelly to get someone across to the Comfort Inn, pronto, adding, "See if Pippa is free; she's good at that kind of thing. Oh and get that evidence bag off Tanner if it's not too late."

Kelly departs while Ruth turns to Paul again.

"We still haven't reached your parents either. They are currently staying in Dubbo, is that correct?"

He nods, a plump tear dropping out of one eye as he does so. "Yeah, they needed to be closer to the hospital, to my grandfather. He's… well, he's the one who's supposed to be…" He doesn't need to finish that sentence.

Ruth nods now. "We do have a mobile number for them, but they're not picking up."

"No, they're useless with their mobile. Never charge it. Probably haven't even switched it on."

Probably haven't even taken it with them, I want to add. Or at least not the Samsung I gave them. I don't know what that iPhone's all about.

"Do you know the name of the hotel where they're staying? Maisie's friends weren't much help there."

"No… Sorry. I can't help you either."

"No ideas at all?"

He shakes his head. Looks stricken.

Great family, you got here, Maisie. Real close, she thinks sarcastically, and I can't blame her.

We used to swap contact numbers and itineraries; we used to know each other's business. When did that stop?

"And you?" she says.

"Me?" He blinks back.

"Where have you been for the past two hours? I had an officer stop at your place on Dulwich Road, and there was no response." *It looked derelict,* she wanted to add but held her tongue.

"Oh, yeah, no, we… we're not on Dulwich anymore. Sale goes through next week. We're at a smaller place now, down on the other side of Chatswood. Shit. No wonder… right."

She frowns and checks her notes. "And your mobile? You weren't answering that either."

He stares at her, still looking so confused. It's like Ruth's talking at chipmunk pace and he can't keep up. Eventually he registers what she says and looks at his mobile again, then clicks something on the side.

"It was on silent." He sighs heavily. "Ruby… our youngest… she's got, well, she's got a bit of a cold. We haven't been getting any sleep. Didn't want to wake the house."

It makes more sense now. A sick kid trumps a dead sister any day I guess.

"So how did you know," Ruth begins. "How did you hear about Maisie?"

He shakes himself as if still trying to keep up, then mumbles something about his wife and breastfeeding and Facebook.

"There was a post, um, about Maisie. Freaked Jan out. She… she woke me. All hysterical. Looked like she'd been to hell and back." He sighs. "I should call her. See if she's all right."

Ruth holds up one palm. "That will have to wait." She drags a chair out and finally takes a seat across from him.

"I know it's a very difficult time, Mr May. I know it's a tremendous shock." She offers him a slim smile. "But I do have some more questions, if you feel up to it."

He drops his head in his hands again and mumbles, "Yeah, sure."

She nods at Kelly who has returned, a plastic bag held low against his thigh.

She says, "I'm sorry but I have to ask, do you have any reason to believe someone might have wanted to harm your sister?"

"*Harm* her?" Paul looks up, the wrinkle between his eyes now a deep ravine. "But I thought… I thought it was suicide."

I want to scream. *Why is everyone so quick to pin it on the victim?*

Ruth watches him for what seems forever, then replies, "At this stage of the investigation, we are treating it as suspicious."

She holds one hand out to Kelly, who places the evidence bag in her palm. It's the gun, of course, and Paul glances at it and away and then back at it again.

"That's Dad's gun," he says, his tone almost matter-of-fact.

She nods. "We assumed as much. It was hanging on the wall in his office? Is that correct? On the two hooks?"

"Um, sure, yeah, I think so." His forehead smooths over. I think he's starting to comprehend even though he says, "I don't understand. What's Dad's pistol got to do with—?" His eyes widen, his lips part. Oh yeah, he gets it now.

"Your sister received a fatal head wound, Mr May."

"*Head wound?*" he repeats.

"She was shot in the head. With this gun, we believe. It's not confirmed yet of course, but it was located close to the body. I'm so sorry."

She's watching him closely now, but if it's signs of guilt she's looking for, she'll be disappointed. Paul seems completely thrown by the revelation, his brow furrowing all over again. It's like a sand dune, that strip between his eyes, rippling with every emotion, giving everything away. His eyes dart back and forth from the gun to the detective and back again.

Finally he says, "Shot? Are you *sure*?"

Ruth looks at him with the patience of a mother. "Yes, it's conclusive."

I can tell Paul's mind is racing away. I can see that from the deepening furrow and the darting eyes and the fact that he's now pulling at his lower lip again (he'd be an atrocious poker player), but I am not privy to his thoughts and it's both exasperating and a little worrying, to be frank. Why doesn't Paul want me to read his mind? What's he hiding from me?

Ruth's thinking the same thing. "Do you know how to use a gun, Mr May? Does your brother?"

He stops torturing his lip and meets her eyes. "Sure. I mean, we did some target practise at the farm, but that was *years* ago. That was with the rifle. Gramps taught me when I was twelve, but... but I've never..." He gulps painfully. "You don't think we... You don't think *I*...? I didn't shoot my sister! I could never do that to Maisie!"

"Which is why I have to ask again. Do you have any reason to believe someone might have wanted to harm your sister?"

Paul snaps himself out of it now. He's heard her loud and clear. As his forehead straightens out, he folds his arms across his chest, sits back in his chair and says. "No. No I do not."

And, sadly for him, Ruth and I don't believe a word of it.

CHAPTER 11

Ruth is called away—something about the office computer and a "suspicious post"—and I am tempted to follow her, but my brother's behaviour is just too extraordinary to dismiss.

He looks dodgy. Why does he look so dodgy? I need to keep watching.

No sooner has she stepped out of the kitchen, he is reaching for his phone again and stabbing at a number. He waits, tapping a fat thumb on the wooden tabletop.

Tap, tap, tap, tap. Tap, tap, tap.

He frowns, starts to hang up, then pulls the phone back to his head quickly and spits into it. "I *knew* you were there! I knew it!"

Then he glances towards the kitchen doorway before whispering, "What the hell did you do? Just tell me. Just *say* it!"

He listens for a second, then says, "Don't act dumb and don't bloody tell me to calm down." Then he does calm down, his voice dropping considerably. I can barely hear him as he says, "We had an agreement. You promised me. You *promised*—"

Then he abruptly hangs up as Ruth walks back in.

I don't know what she says to him then. I have no clue.

Suddenly I am whirling through time and space. I am shuffling down the hallway in my pyjamas, from the direction of the study. I am thinking, *Someone needs to vacuum that crap off the carpet*, but I don't have the heart or the energy to do it. I can hear voices.

Someone says, "It is what it is, mate; we have to suck it up," but the voice is slightly muffled. It's coming from the kitchen. It's another day, another time. The sun is shining, the birds are chirping, the anguish in the tone is incongruous.

"But he can't do that! We had an agreement! He *promised*!" It's a man's voice, clearer now. My brother Peter, I think, but I didn't realise he was back from London yet.

"Tell me about it! Jan's spewing. She's irate!" That's Paul, equally as vexed. I haven't heard that tone in months.

There's a pause, then "What's Jan got to do with it?"

What? I think. *What are they talking about?* I stop just outside the door and keep listening.

"It's got everything to do with Jan! Jesus, we've been stone broke for years, we're selling our home for Christ's sake, moving into a friggin' shoebox with four kids, and he's just gonna sell Nevercloud on a whim? For *her*? Without even thinking about it!"

Another pause and then Peter sighs loudly, but his tone has calmed considerably as he says, "I'm sure he's thought about it, Paul. I'm sure that's *all* he can think about. That's the problem; he's not thinking straight. We need to tell him. That's all."

There's a scoff. "What do we tell him, mate? 'You can't do it, Dad! She's just not worth it!'?"

There is silence. It seems to go on forever, and then finally Paul speaks again, his tone back to placatory.

"You're right. He loves her; what else can he do?" Then, to book end the conversation, he says, "It is what it bloody is."

I waited a few minutes, then strode casually into the kitchen and feigned innocence as I smiled at my two brothers who stood at opposite ends, arms wrapped around their chests, cheeks ruddy.

"Hey, guys," I said. "What's up?"

"Nothing," they replied in unison, clearly hiding something.

I smiled at them like a shark. I remember that. I was super patient. I knew I'd get it out of them. Eventually.

I was a big fan of games like hide-and-seek when I was a kid. I could play it all day for hours. My brothers loathed it, or at least they came to loathe it, so persistent was my passion. As the youngest in the family I was also the smallest, which meant more hidey-holes were open to me than my taller, lankier siblings, and they got so incensed when they couldn't find me.

I hid above the fridge once, in a cupboard half-filled with brilliantly coloured bottles. Spirits and liqueurs I realised much later. How I got up there and how I managed to squeeze in amongst the Galliano and the Cointreau is anyone's guess, but I was good like that, a champion hider. And I had the patience of a predator. Happy to wait it out.

Of course, eventually, frequently, the boys gave up on finding me and headed back to their bedrooms, but that didn't worry me. I just waited until one of them reappeared to fetch a drink and then burst down upon them, causing them to shriek.

I always won that game. I really liked winning.

My brothers fought frequently, but the one thing they agreed on was that I was annoying. They were united in their loathing of me. I mean, I'm not playing the sympathy card here. I know they loved me, love me still, but they found me so aggravating, like my simple presence sent red-hot bolts of anger through them both. They said it was because I was bossy and told lame jokes at dinner and was "a spoiled little shit." They said Mum and Dad treated me differently. But I think it had more to do with the fact that it gave them something to unite against, otherwise they had nothing.

Peter and Paul may sound like a unified team, all Christian-like, but they never really had time for each other. They loathed me from time to time, but it was each other they really despised.

Tessa used to call them Stork and Sleaze, a less polite version of Chalk and Cheese. One was a homebody, mad about babies, the other a playboy, mad about babes. That was Peter, of course, the eldest, the one who lives in London and stays in strange hotels and is still missing in action.

Peter is thirty-five going on fifteen. Apart from the adult job—he's an obscenely overpaid banker—he'll never grow up. Doesn't want to. Makes no apologies for it either. Dad had hoped he'd settle down, maybe even run the farm, thought he had a knack for it, but that never happened, and I guess that's when Uncle Simon stepped up.

I know Dad regrets that. I know he would like to live at Nevercloud permanently, himself, Mum not so much. So to hear they might be selling the place makes me sit up and take notice. Why would they be selling it? Did Mum force Dad's hand?

As for Paul? He wanted a wife and kids before he was twenty, and he almost got his wish. His eldest, Meg, is about ten or eleven, and he's just turned thirty-three.

I think he's happy.

I thought he was happy.

I thought a lot of things once.

Paul's one of those people who'll always just *get by*. His face might resemble a quivering sand dune, but he won't leave any footsteps on the beach, he won't cause any waves, and he won't hurt anyone, or at least I didn't think he would. He works for the council, in a clerical position of some sort. I'm embarrassed to say I can't tell you precisely what. Every time it came up, I just glazed over.

I always assumed it was the perfect job for Paul

though: nine-to-five, rostered days off, set job requirements, stable salary. And, being government-based, very, very difficult to get fired from. Knowing Paul as I did, he only ever would have put in just enough effort to stay on the right side of the annual performance review, but maybe he hasn't put in nearly enough effort lately, maybe he's on strike two.

Or did he lose the unlosable job? Is that why he's in such financial straits?

His wife Jan's no use, of course. She's a stay-at-home mum, which I'd normally admire except she never actually left the home, even before the kids came along. She's just always sat on the couch and waited for Paul to bring home the bacon. And now, it seems, the bacon has turned to the budget cuts.

Why did I not know that? Did they not tell me, or was I too entrenched in my own problems to really notice?

Now as I watch Paul standing at the kitchen sink, a fingerprint analyst smudging his thumbs onto a plastic-coated sheet while he thinks only of his wife, I can't help but wonder.

When did Paul become so broke he had to downsize? Why did he never tell me life had become so tough? I'm sure I would've remembered if he had, just like I know I never did find out exactly what he and Peter were talking about that day in the kitchen, despite my earlier confidence.

"Have you flipped your lid?" Paul said, his voice as fake as the cream in my cake when I asked him about it later. "Dad's not selling Nevercloud. Don't worry, little sis, you must have misheard us."

But I know what I heard, and it's his deceit that has me worried.

Then out of the blue something hits me like a second bullet through the brain. I can't believe it hadn't occurred to me earlier. As I watch Paul wipe his inky fingers on a paper towel, I start to wonder: Where are my parents?

Why aren't they answering that stupid iPhone?

How long does it take for news to reach them, for them to scramble for the car and get back on the highway? Surely *someone* has spoken to them by now? Surely someone has asked them to come home?

There's a chill running down my spine, or it would be if I still had one.

Oh God. Please don't tell me my beloved parents are lying somewhere, bullets in their heads, their hair as messy as mine.

Before I can give that horrifying thought more oxygen, an engine roars to life and shakes me back to reality.

Okay, Maisie, deep breaths. No point getting hysterical. At least not yet.

I drop the ugly images and continue to look down.

Outside, the last of the revellers are leaving, and I am glad of the distraction. I see Roco wave a hand out of his Corolla window to Leslie and Jonas, who wave back, Leslie's car keys tinkling as she does so.

Roco has Tessa in the passenger seat, and I am sadly not surprised. She looks very comfortable there. Like she belongs. And Una is trudging along the street, hands wrapped around her belly, shoulders hunched.

"Need a lift?" Leslie calls out, beeping her SUV to life as she does so.

"It's one block, you lazy buggers," she calls back. "Pretty sure I'll be safe."

Then I watch as both cars accelerate away and she reaches for her phone again, her expression desolate. It doesn't last long. The second her screen lights up, her eyes follow suit. She stops in her tracks, turns swiftly around and starts striding towards my house. Then her footsteps slow down, she stops again, hesitating momentarily before turning once again and resuming her walk away. She's confused or tentative or torn.

Or something.

After a few more strides, Una stops yet again, but this time she pulls her phone towards her and stabs at the screen a few times.

Then she places it to one ear and I hear her say, "Oh, *David*," before everything goes silent.

CHAPTER 12

My first thought is one of overwhelming relief. I feel myself exhale, my spine thaw out. Okay, good. My parents are fine. *Of course* they're fine. What was I thinking!

If Una is talking to my dad—and I have to assume she is, judging by the river of tears streaming down her face—that means he's alive and kicking, and Mum must be by his side.

Then a second thought wrestles its way in. Why is Una's conversation with my father hidden from me? I know I'm dead. She knows I'm dead. What's there to hide?

I watch more keenly as Una gives up walking completely and slumps down onto the sidewalk, her long legs folded into the gutter, her voice still hidden, her sobbing intensifying. She'll short-circuit her device if she doesn't stop.

Her tears should be comforting to me, so why do I suddenly feel like a dirty old man, peering through the curtains at the naked chick in the next apartment? Why should I feel like the intruder when it's me they're talking about?

Or is it?

I give myself another shake. What else could Una and my dad be discussing?

Come on, Maisie, now you're just being odd. This is a good thing! My parents must have given Una their new number—for whatever reason, let's not complicate things—and now at least they're in the loop. Now they can pull together and sort it all out. And I know exactly how things will play out. They'll pull on some clothes, throw their suitcase in the car, then get straight back on the highway and be home in four hours.

They'll be devastated, of course they will, but together they'll work out who did this to me. Together they'll help solve my murder.

Except...

Well, when it comes to my parents, *together* is not a word that suits them these days. My parents haven't exactly been a unified force of late, not like the old days when their love traversed time and space. And I mean that quite literally—Dad was pushing forty and lived in the country, Mum was a city girl who'd just turned twenty-five.

Have we got time for a little detour? I think it might help.

You see, my folks first met in a paddock near Gilgandra, not far from Dad's property, at a Bachelor and Spinster Ball. That's just a big ole barn dance, really, where single country folk dress up, drink up and hook up if they're lucky.

Except my parents didn't just hook up, they fell in love. And I always assumed that Dad must have fallen harder because even though they met in the outback, he was the one who ditched the dust for the Big Smoke, following her all the way to Sydney. Mandy had a thriving career at an insurance firm in the city at that time. She gave it all up when she had me. I never did understand that. I didn't really respect it either, if I'm being honest. There was never any question that Mum would settle in Dubbo— "I just wasn't country stock"—and I guess he never pushed her. Maybe he never asked.

Apart from that one-off trip to the country—a friend dragged her along, she wasn't even going to go—Mum couldn't abide the rural life, told anyone who'd listen, and so Dad had to suck it up I guess and pour his love of the land into a landscaping business that proved lucrative enough. But I know he was unsettled. I've always felt his detachment, like a mighty oak reduced to weed status because it happens to be rooted in the wrong place. And, to be honest, I never really cared. Selfish of me, I know, but I was with Mum on that one. I didn't mind the odd visit to the dustbowl they called Dubbo, but I didn't want to live out there! Yikes. *Imagine the social life!*

The suggestion to return to Nevercloud came up from time to time, usually on the long drive home from visiting Gramps, when they thought I was fast asleep in the back. Dad would always bring it up, and Mum would always hear him out.

"You know I love it out here, don't you, dear? You know I miss the old place."

"Yes, love, I know."

"You know the kids would love it too, especially the boys, especially Peter."

"Oh, they'd die of boredom, Peter more than any of them!" She'd scoff, and I'd silently high-five her from the back.

"It'd do him some good."

"He can do good in London, love."

Dad would scoff at that. He didn't have much time for bankers; it was banks who were always nipping at the heels of poor country folk, repossessing properties that had been in families for generations, providing the final straw for breakdowns and suicides and all that violin-playing stuff. That's what Mum would scoff at. She didn't blame the banks, and neither did I. They might be evil behemoths with all the power, but even they couldn't make it rain. You couldn't blame them for the drought.

"I'm just saying, Peter would be… well, he'd be *better* in the bush. He'd be happier, more settled."

This was usually the stage where Mum would sigh and say something like "This is about *you*, David, so let's not pretend it's about the kids. This is about you being happier and more settled."

"And what the bloody hell is wrong with that?" he'd snap back, his voice as dark as the crows above the rotting carcasses we passed. Then he'd say something like "I've got roots out here, you can't ignore that. You can't just wish that away."

I'd hold my breath while Mum would steady hers before answering carefully, firmly, "I don't wish that away, David. I visit Nevercloud every single time you ask me to, and so do the kids. We don't particularly enjoy it, but we've never denied you that. It's not just about you though, is it? It's about all of us. *Our* roots are in Sydney. They have been here for decades."

By the time we reach the outskirts of the city, Dad would have lapsed into a sullen silence and Mum would be breathing a little easier, but I knew each bout, as benign as they seemed, took something from them, left them feeling a little bruised and bloody, their marriage a little more battered.

Is that why Dad was thinking of selling Nevercloud? Was he finally throwing in the towel? Had Mum finally insisted upon it, or was he doing it to patch up their marriage?

As I watch Una continue to talk and sob and sniffle and sigh, wondering what the hell she could be saying to her friend's dad for so long, an image of the soft pink envelope pops into my mind, followed by the furtive look on Vijay's face as he tried to get Una's attention in the laneway.

I start to join dots that really shouldn't go together, that make my stomach turn, when a loud voice calls out.

"The sneaky bastards!"

For a moment there I think that voice is commiserating with me, but then I realise there's a new commotion going on, down in the guest bathroom by the pool, and this time

Officer Craig is at the centre of it. He's standing by the door watching as a SOCO with receding orange hair holds something over the cistern while it drips.

It's a ziplock bag with a white box inside. Looks like more medication to me.

"Drugs?" Craig says, eyes alight.

"Better," the SOCO replies, reaching into his pocket for a fresh evidence bag. "*Illegal* drugs."

Craig beams from one giant ear to the other.

CHAPTER 13

I give myself a shake. Okay, time to concentrate.

A bag of illegal drugs has just been found stashed in the outside toilet, and it's far more pressing, me thinks. I don't know what Una is up to or what that pink envelope signifies, but I need to get my priorities in order, and my friend's bizarre behaviour cannot be one of them nor can my parents' shaky marriage.

I watch now as the redhead drops the tablets into the evidence bag, zips it up and then pulls out a marker pen to scribble something on the front.

"Can I show the DI?" Craig asks, and he shrugs, handing it over.

"Just get it straight back to me. I have to process it."

Craig nods, then heads back into the house, looking for Ruth.

I could point him in the right direction. She is now back in Dad's office, seated at his desk, staring at his computer, Kelly standing behind her.

They both have steaming mugs in hand like they're on a tea break and are just checking their Twitter feed. Ruth's cup smells suspiciously like liquorice. Someone has clearly found my mother's stash of herbal tea and whipped up some refreshments. Mum never even drank herbal tea until I moved back home. Now she has peppermint and chamomile and sleepytime and, yes, of all flavours, liquorice. She says she bought them for me, but I know differently. I know they help her relax, and I am sad that I made her so tense.

Ruth brings the cup to her nose, smelling the aniseed. It used to make me gag, that smell, but she is breathing it in like it's a blood transfusion.

"So what do you think?" Kelly asks, dabbing a peppermint tea bag in and out, in and out. It doesn't really go with his whole surfer dude veneer.

"I think mischief is afoot," is her cryptic reply.

"I hate to break it to you, boss, but it *could* just be suicide, you know? As boring as that is."

"Nah," says Ruth. "There's something else going on here. I can smell it."

Good, I think. *Don't let that herbal tea turn your brain to mush.*

"You think they want us to *think* it was suicide?" says Kelly.

She shrugs. "I think they're up to something."

For the first time, I notice an object in Ruth's other hand. It's thin and white, and she's tapping the keyboard with it. Tappity, tap, tap.

What is that?

Ah yes, the Qantas boarding pass I saw earlier tonight. Now that's piqued my interest. Qantas is an international airline, right? That pass must be ancient. Unless it belongs to my wanderlust brother, the last overseas trip my parents took was a week in Vanuatu with us kids, over a decade ago. I was seventeen, just out of school, the boys in their twenties. So why has it suddenly reappeared? Has someone been reminiscing, I wonder?

"Maybe I'm overcomplicating things," Ruth says now, and Kelly nods. He's thought that since the beginning, hence all the eye rolling.

Blowing a puff of air through his lips, "That post does kind of sum it up."

They both stare back at the screen, and I try to follow their eyes, but that Facebook page still looks like a dog's breakfast to me, all jumbled and messy.

If I'm following the rules correctly, and I think I am, it's clear whoever posted something on that page does not want me to read it.

"Boss?" This is Craig, holding the evidence bag between a thumb and forefinger like it's contaminated with faeces. Oh for goodness' sake. It's a fresh bag. It never even got close.

She looks up at it and scowls. "What did I tell you, Craig? We're not vice."

"This is related. I'm sure of it."

Her eyes squint. "What?"

He names a drug that sounds a lot like a party upper to me, and her whole demeanour changes. She looks first excited, then, oddly, disappointed, and I wonder what's disappointing her so much.

"Bugger it," she says, sounding weary. "Where?"

"SOCOs found it in the pool toilet. In the cistern."

"Of course they did. Got a name on it? Any clues who put it there." He shakes his head. "Okay, get it back to them, and see if they can get prints."

Kelly looks confused; he's not keeping up. "You think someone tried to drug her first? Knock her out?"

Ruth's not listening, she's tapping a text into her phone, and I can read this one. (Thanks for throwing me a few scraps, Ruth!)

It's for Michaelia, and it says, "Need tox results ASAP."

Good idea, woman, and about time too. Let's see who tried to drug me before they put a bullet in my head. It might help explain why my voice was slurring and why I was so shaky on my feet.

"Sounds like a bit of overkill to me," comes a churlish tone by my side, and I swing around to find Neal hovering.

"Shouldn't you be lurking in the dark where you belong?" I spit out.

"Just checking in."

"Just eavesdropping on something that's none of your business, you mean."

"Still in a delightful mood I see."

"Hey, I didn't ask for this, okay? Why should I be happy?"

He looks to the heavens. "It's going to be a very *loooong* night."

Than he vanishes as quickly as he appeared, his snigger lingering after him.

Back inside, a phone is ringing again, its tone shrill and urgent. It's funny the way phones sound more desperate the later the night gets.

It's Craig's ringtone—I recognise it from last time—and it's coming from the kitchen where he left it. He takes off to retrieve it while Ruth and Kelly return to staring sullenly at Dad's computer.

"They're hiding something," Ruth says apropos of nothing, and Kelly nods again.

He knows what she's talking about this time, and he agrees there is something suspicious going on. I'm surprised he's abandoned the suicide angle so quickly. Those drugs must be very telling.

"Reckon they'll 'fess up?"

Not sure I want them to, Ruth thinks to herself, her lips remaining in a thin, grim line as she shrugs. "Probably not. Would you?"

That shakes me a bit. How can she say that? It's her *job* to know, whether she wants to hear the truth or not.

Kelly appears to be on my wavelength because he says, "Doesn't matter who they are, if they've had anything to do with this, we can throw the book at them."

She nods, thinking, *You're so young, Kelly. That's your problem.*

"And you're old and jaded!" I want to scream down to her. "Just do your freakin' job!"

"Where did the brother go?" Ruth says now, her tone back to weary. "I guess we better get him in here for another chat, see if he can explain any of this."

I don't know exactly what she's referring to—the drugs? The Facebook post?—but I do know where Paul is. I can see him right now, standing at the bottom of the driveway, hands on his hips, a smudge of black ink across his jeans.

He's clearly waiting for someone, and whoever it is, he looks both terrified and furious. You can just imagine the state of his forehead!

While I watch Paul frown and sigh and continue massacring his lip, I hear the distant plucking of a guitar and the melancholy tones of English songwriter Nick Drake. He's singing about time and what it's told him. *Not to ask for more*, by the sounds of things.

Gee, I could have told Nick that!

There's another party going on, a more mournful one than mine. The key players have shifted to Tessa's house, and I wonder if I can shift across. My line of sight is like a circle rippling out from that front office where I died. My carcass may be gone, but that spot is clearly my anchor. I can't seem to dislocate from it. Having said that, I can lean out, away from that bloodied carpet and across to the McGee's where Roco's and Leslie's cars are now parked out the front.

Tessa's place is just like ours, minus the fancy renovations. The gaudy pillars are still there and the ugly tangerine bricks, and there's also an unkempt front lawn, which rarely find its way below a mower. My dad used to mow it when Tessa's father first took off, then Peter and then Paul, and now, who knows? I guess Dad still wanders over and fires up the rusty old "pushie" whenever he finds the energy. Or maybe another neighbour has taken over, although not lately by the looks of it.

Inside, I can see Tessa's mum, Tammie, sitting on the lumpy couch in the corner of their lounge room, looking like a child at a horror movie. Her eyes are wide, her lips are parted, her fingers trembling at her neck as she listens to Tessa's retelling of my murder. She's clearly just been dragged from bed as her dyed yellow hair is still smooched up from her pillow and her body cloaked in a terry-towelling dressing gown.

Beside her sits Una, and Roco is perched on the edge of a mismatched armchair, while Jonas and Leslie and Arabella all loll on the floor, looking dog-tired yet hyperactive. The adrenaline is clearly still flowing.

"The kettle's boiled," calls someone from the kitchen, and now I feel like I'm in a horror flick.

It's Mr Tall, Dark and Handsome.

When did Vijay Singh get so firmly entrenched in my life? Or is it my death that has cemented his presence? They chorus out their thanks, and then Tessa's mum staggers to her feet, taking orders. She's been the caretaker for so long she goes on automatic pilot. Three hot chocolates, two green teas and a strong coffee, thanks.

It's almost three in the morning, and everybody is enjoying a soothing cup of something while my body lies cold on a slab somewhere and a cold-blooded killer gets away with murder.

Why is no one thinking about that?

Why is no one worried that a madman is running loose? Someone who had the gall to take a gun and shoot me dead in the middle of a party?

As if reading my vibes, Arabella says, "Is anyone else feeling a little freaked? I mean, what if the killer is still around? What if he's someone from the party?"

Tessa and Roco share a look, and Una stares at her boots.

"Oh don't be so melodramatic," says Jonas. "She *obviously* did this to herself. For God's sake, you're such a drama queen." Then he frowns and adds, haughtily, "Anyway, why do you assume it's a man?"

"I don't. It's just… well, guns are so *violent* aren't they?

They're so *male.*"

"Nah, knives are much more violent," says Leslie. "Guns are quite efficient, when you think about it. Quite detached. An ideal weapon for a woman. No need for strength, no need even for close proximity. Just a quick bang and they're dead."

Now all eyes are upon her, and Roco's are blazing.

"What?" says Leslie. "I'm just saying."

"Well don't *just say*. Jesus, Les," says Roco. "She was our friend!"

"I know," says Leslie, while I think, er, actually Roco darling, I was your *girlfriend*. But what's a name change between lovers?

I still haven't gotten to the bottom of that. If what he says is true—and I'm pretty sure it's not—when did we break up? And why would we do that? I don't remember a single fight. Not one. So I guess it all comes back to Tessa.

"The police will work it all out," she says now.

Again, I assume she's talking to me until I hear Una think to herself, *That's what I'm worried about.*

When I was twelve I broke my arm in a trampoline accident. Well, it wasn't an accident so much as a really stupid mistake. Bored with the same old bouncy, bouncy, bounce, Tessa and I toppled the trampoline onto its side and then threw ourselves up and off it, kamikaze-style. I'm not sure why we thought that would be a good idea, but I ended up smashing into the legs and hearing my elbow crack against the rusty metal.

We were at Tessa's place, and Mrs McGee went *berserk*, but I knew then, even at that age, that it wasn't me she was worried about. It was her reputation as a mother. I had broken my arm on her watch.

I knew my parents would be cool with it. I knew they wouldn't blame her one bit, but the way Tammie went on and on about how silly I was and how naughty and goodness didn't I have more brains than that?

Tessa and I sniggered all the way to the hospital, me tensing at the rolling pain, Tessa rolling her eyes at her mother.

That's kind of how everyone is acting tonight. Like my death is less about me and more about them. Is that what they're all worried about? Is that what they're hiding? The simple fact that I died on their watch and nobody was able to save me. They were too busy partying to protect their best friend. And now they all have to live with that. They have to front up to the police and my parents and whoever else bothers to ask and admit that I was shot in cold blood while they were laughing and drinking and splashing about or, in Arabella's case, hooking up with God-knows-who in Peter's old bed?

Or is it something else? Is it darker than that?

Do *they* have something to do with it? I wouldn't have thought so once upon a time, but the way they're all acting—including my brother who's now pacing the street like he's got a full bladder—well, all I can hear are alarm bells, folks, but nobody seems to have woken up to it yet.

Perhaps it's time to get our thoughts straight. Perhaps it's time for a recap. I know at least some of the cops (well, Kelly mostly) and at least one friend (yes, Jonas, I'm looking at you) are clinging to the suicide angle like a life raft, and who can blame them? The idea is a little too tempting to discount. It's certainly the easiest option for everybody; gets them all off the hook. And if you think about it, logically it does make sense.

I *did* have antidepressants by my bedside. That has to be conceded. They did have my name on them. You don't need to look.

I *was* forced to move home after losing my job, although why I lost it has yet to be explored; there *has* to be more to it than a few smashed cups.

And I *may* even have been dumped by my boyfriend while he slept with my BFF. (He's denied me twice now, did you notice that?)

So, yes, there *were* a few reasons to be depressed, but I'm pretty sure I wouldn't do that to my folks, and I'm confident those newfound drugs are giving Ruth, for one, something fresh to grab on to. She wants to know who hid them and why and what, if anything, they have to do with my death.

She also wants to know more about Vijay Singh and has just given belated instructions to Black Bob to look him up. I'm curious about him too, the way he's ingratiated himself into my life, but I'm even more curious about my brother.

Paul has stopped wearing out the pavement and is now staring expectantly at a vehicle that's crawling up our street like it's a taxi and it's lost.

Actually, I'm not far off. It's an Uber. I can tell from the small sticker on the driver's side of the rear windscreen, and I'm guessing it's electric because it's barely purring; so quiet in fact that no one inside notices, not even Door Bitch who's chatting to someone at the end of the laneway.

I keep watching the car, intrigued as it comes to a stop in the middle of the road, just a few houses down. Who would turn up at this ungodly hour and in an electric-powered Uber at that? My parents wouldn't even have the ridesharing app, let alone want to pay for one all the way from the Central West.

It must be someone else.

No, make that *something* else—a thick black something that is slipping out of the passenger side and now hovering towards my brother, the vehicle barely visible through all that black.

It looks like a mass of locusts, a shimmering evil splotch.

It sends another icy trickle down my spine.

I want to scream at Paul. I want to tell him to run and hide, but he does quite the opposite. He starts walking towards the car, then running, and is suddenly swallowed up inside all that ghastly black.

CHAPTER 14

After several terrifying minutes, Paul reappears, stepping out of the darkness and back under the streetlight, his face wet, his eyes red and puffy. His anger has dissolved, and he just looks, well, shattered.

"I know," he mumbles, wiping a hand across his nose and slathering snot up his right cheek. "I can't believe it either, but... but then how did it happen? How did she end up like that?"

He waits for a response, one that's beyond my ears, but I know he's getting his answer because the splotch is shimmering wildly while Paul shakes his head. There's obviously a person hidden in that darkness, and I think I know who it is. Have you guessed yet? I just don't understand the secrecy. I don't understand any of this!

After a minute or so I hear Paul's tone rise an octave. "So where is it then? What did you do with it?"

The smudge shimmers again, and Paul's eyes glance up the driveway, towards the house.

"Are you mad? Why did you leave it there?" He stops, listens, snarls suddenly, his temper back at boiling point. "You bloody relax! This is a big deal. I don't think you get that. We could end up in gaol, mate." Silence then, "No... no!" Then, "Well who then?" and "Bullshit! There's no way that happened!"

He is shaking his head and so am I. I may only have half the conversation, but it's obvious they're discussing the drugs Craig just found, and it's clear they are somehow involved.

"Mr May! Is that you down there? Paul May?"

Paul swings around with a start. Constable Craig is standing halfway down the driveway, his eyes squinting at the shadow. "Is that... Is that your brother, Mr May?"

Paul releases a long sigh, then strides back towards the house while my oldest brother follows behind him, lost in his own ugly shadow.

"Nice of you to show up eventually, Peter!" I yell down at him. Pity you can't hear me and pity you haven't got the balls to show your face.

Then I turn my percolating anger towards the tunnel.

"What is going on?" I scream into the abyss. "Why is everybody hiding from me? Why all the secrets?"

The tunnel remains dark, infuriatingly silent.

Where is Deseree? Where is that dickhead Neal? Hell, I'll take Emie if I have to! I just need some answers!

I take a deep breath. I exhale.

Calm down, Maisie, you've got this, says a voice in my head, a younger voice, yet it sounds a million years old. I take another breath, then I do the only thing I can do. I force myself to keep watching.

My treacherous brother is now hovering in the kitchen, an officer almost blacked out by his shadow, while Paul makes his way to the edge of the pool, looking like he wants to throw himself in. But he doesn't. Of course he doesn't. He was never one for grand gestures or theatrics. Take it from me, people, his earlier outbursts were uncharacteristic.

Now he just stands there, wraps his arms around himself and looks constipated.

Meanwhile, Craig is back at the office door, his face flushed like a preschooler with the best show-and-tell. Ever.

"Two quick things, ma'am," he tells Ruth, his words tumbling on top of each other. "We've located the second brother, the one that went missing. Peter May." He pauses, sucks in some air. "He's in the kitchen now. SOCOs are taking prints."

Ruth barely glances up from the screen she's been studying. She's not so impressed. "I hope you separated them," she mumbles. "The brothers, I mean." Then she darts her eyes at Craig. "Please tell me you did that."

He nods gleefully; he's not as green as he looks.

"And the second thing?"

His glee turns psychotic. "We've also found the parents! Just spoke with my mate in Dubbo. They're on their way back. Halfway home."

"Already?"

"Yes! Somebody must have got word to them or something because they're only a few hours away."

"Well done, Craig," she says, but he doesn't get any gold stars on his forehead from me.

Una was obviously the person who got through to my folks; we already know that. One of her earlier texts must have forced them out of their cosy slumber and onto the highway. By the time she'd finally spoken to Dad, I'm guessing they were well on their way back. Or at least that's what it sounds like.

"Explains why the Dubbo crew couldn't find them, I guess," says Craig.

"I guess," she says. "That's a relief."

I'm more worried about myself, to be honest. I know that sounds selfish and I'm glad my parents are returning, but I'm not sure I have the strength to hang around and watch it all unfold. I might be dead, but I'm still human.

Do I really need to see the two people I love most deal with my murder and its aftermath? Is that what Forever wants to inflict upon me?

Am I in hell? Is that it? Did I bring this upon myself? Do I deserve to watch their misery while others get to cross over quietly and move on to the afterlife?

I already told you, I know how this will play out.

I know my mother will be distraught and my father stony-faced and silent. But I can't help feeling there'll be some guilt in the mix, and I'm not sure I understand why. And what of my brothers? Will Peter ever show his face to me again?

Why does he feel the need to mask himself? What is he hiding?

Perhaps it's time to shine a light on Pete. We're highlighting all the potential suspects, so why should he miss out? He's acting the dodgiest of all.

You haven't met Peter yet, at least not properly. You haven't seen his face. He's a good-looking man, always was the better looking of the brothers. I wonder if that's why Paul decided to marry the first girl he met because he never expected to do any better and why Pete can't help but splash his good looks about, knowing it won't last.

He was such a party boy, too, our Pete. Went through a terribly rebellious stage, expelled from one school and caught twice with Ecstasy, once at a music festival, another time while underage at a nightclub. Dad wanted to ship him off to Gramps, stick him in the middle of nowhere and give him a wake-up call, but Mum wouldn't hear of it. She needed him close. Hugs and home cooking, remember? They were her remedy. And, like the topic of Nevercloud, Pete's antics became a thorn in their already prickly relationship.

They argued over it so often I grew to despise my brother, and I remember bursting into his room one day, waking him from a deep sleep, and demanding he stop being such a knucklehead. I was probably about ten, so you'll forgive the lingo.

"You're ruining everything!" I said, my voice low, lest I set off another parental argument. "You need to start being a bit nicer, please."

"Oh piss off, Maisie," was his only response before he turned over and hid beneath his duvet.

That's when I set about trying to save him. I watched shows where naughty kids were sent away to be straightened out by stern strangers, and I picked up brochures on schizophrenia and ADHD and behavioural management "issues." I didn't have the slightest clue what was wrong with Peter; I just needed it to be fixed. I knew if I could somehow solve it, everything would be fine again. We could all go back to normal; Mum and Dad would have one less thing to fight about.

And then somehow, irrespective of all that, it fixed itself. Pete stumbled into the stock market and found he had a knack, and the next thing you know he's climbing the corporate ladder and straightening himself out, then getting a job in London and moving away entirely.

But now I have to wonder about those drugs the SOCOs found stashed down the toilet and whether they belonged to Pete.

Is he back to his old tricks? Or has he never stopped?

More importantly, did I catch him with the drugs and go ballistic. Perhaps I had flashbacks of that awful time when we were kids, perhaps I didn't "piss off" this time and let him get away with it. Perhaps, this time, it set off a violent argument.

I know it all sounds so ridiculous—my brother wouldn't shoot me, surely?—but he has a history of drug use and he's the one who fled the scene before my body was discovered. He's also the one who hid for hours not answering his mobile. And he's the one—the only one—who cannot bring himself to show me his face.

Una may be hiding her words, but it's Peter who's acting like a killer.

CHAPTER 15

"Stop it, you're killing me."

This is Tessa, and she doesn't sound at all threatened. She's whispering to Roco, a sneaky smile on her lips, yet unlike others, she's clearly happy for me to listen in.

Is she being cruel or just inconsiderate?

They're at the back door of her house now, cigarettes in hand, and all he's doing is looking at her. Just staring straight at her while she blushes crimson under his gaze. And I can't quite bring myself to blame her. It's like his eyes contain a hundred volts of electricity that's zinging off her and back again.

I can feel the zap from up here—can you feel it? For the first time in my life I understand chemistry. Wow, they really *do* have something, don't they? I never realised.

How long did they feel it? Have they been hiding it from me? Or have they already acted upon it, the surge too strong to resist?

"You got the message?" he says, and her face crumples a little.

"You know I did."

"What do you think?"

Her eyes slide away, and she stares down at her cigarette. "I think it feels like a betrayal."

"But Maisie—"

"I think Maisie would be gutted if she were here now, Roco. I think it's a very tense time. I don't think

92

anyone's thinking straight."

She's looking at him now, and he's nodding as he drags on his smoke. He exhales and says, "We'll wait a bit then."

Sure you will, I think. I'll give you a day or two before you're ripping each other's clothes off. I know I should still be jealous, bursting with recriminations and rage, yet *this* seems so inevitable, like my death is the only holdup.

A burst of giggling erupts from inside. It's Leslie, flirting with Jonas again.

"Want me to get rid of the others?" he says, his thick eyebrows shooting up and down, and Tessa is looking at him sideways again.

"It's not going to happen, Roco. At least not tonight."

Now he blushes, and I wish it was from a smack across the face. It might all be inevitable, but I'm not even in the ground yet, mate.

As if overhearing me, he says, "I'm not talking about that... Jesus, Tess." He sweeps a hand through his hair, looks sheepish. "I just mean, well, how annoying is Leslie tonight? And Jonas. What a dickhead."

"I thought he was your new bromance."

"Was, until I realised he was a wanker. Why didn't you tell me?"

She shrugs, drags on her cigarette. "Most people work it out eventually." She blows out a plume of smoke. "What made you twig?"

"Something he said the other day, something about Maisie." He sniffs. "About why they never stuck. He's a prick."

Not that you can talk, Roco darling, I think.

She nods. "Yep, the king of them."

"You gonna warn Leslie off? She's obviously got the hots for 'Hottie'."

Tessa's eyes squint, and it's not from the smoke. "I thought Leslie was annoying you tonight."

"Yeah, but she doesn't deserve *him*. No one does."

Then Tessa nods vigorously like they're talking about Ted Bundy.

I haven't got time to keep listening or even digest what it is they're discussing because I am drawn back home, back to the pool where some splashing has started up.

Paul is now dangling his naked feet in the water, kicking them up and down like a toddler might, and someone is sitting beside him, her legs scrunched up into her chest watching him. It's Paul's wife, Jan. When did she show up?

"I'm gonna miss her," says Paul, "as infuriating as she could be."

Jan smiles sadly. "Me too, even though she couldn't stand the sight of me."

"She *liked* you!" he rails, but we both know that's not true.

We all know I wasn't Jan's biggest fan. I found her a *bit much*.

My brother is married to the nicest woman in the world. On paper. She's all smiley and earth motherly and stuff, but it's those exact same traits that make you want to smack her across the mouth. And she's boring. Breathtakingly, unforgivably dull. Like I said before, she has no career to speak of, and the way she rabbits on and on about those kids, like no one's ever reproduced before and isn't she a champion? Well, that crap wears thin very quickly when you don't have kids, I can tell you that. But for the most part, we got along fine and I know she adores my lump of a brother. I know that much. So why did she make my skin crawl?

My mother always said I loved my big brothers too much to ever accept a woman in their lives, and it was certainly not an issue I had to worry about with Peter— as you know, he had scores of women, but they never lasted long enough to get to home base.

Paul only ever had Jan.

Is *that* why I disliked her, I wonder now? Because she lassoed my brother before he had a chance to live his life? Or was it because she dragged him away from me and our games of hide-and-seek?

"We should've put her up," says Jan now, peeling her sandals off and dipping her toes tentatively into the water. "We should have insisted she come live with us."

Paul looks incredulous at that. "I thought you didn't want to."

"I didn't! I didn't think it'd be fair to the kids, and God knows we don't have the space, but now..." She sighs. "Maybe if we had."

"Maybe she'd have a bullet through her head in our living room! In front of our kids!"

Jan shudders. "You think? Really?" Then she frowns, swallows, turns to face him. "You didn't have anything to do with..." She falters. "Please tell me you didn't."

His jaw drops; he looks outraged.

"Sorry," she says quickly, "it's just the way you and Peter were talking the other night... I... I thought."

"No! Never! I couldn't! I wouldn't. I'm not like that!" And then, glancing around, he drops his voice and says, "You didn't say anything to the cops, did you?"

She rolls her eyes. "Of course not."

"Because I didn't."

"What about Peter?"

He clenches his lips shut.

"Paul?" she says, horrified.

"I don't know, honey, I honestly don't know. But I didn't! You have to believe me."

"I *do* believe you," she whispers. She bumps his shoulder with her own and then says something rather curious. "You don't have the guts, my love."

He looks at her again, but he's less outraged now than wounded. He looks like he's just been stabbed through the heart.

I remember the exact moment when Paul and Jan skipped into the lounge room and told my parents they were getting hitched. I was just thirteen, and I was bitterly disappointed. It was a Saturday evening, and we were halfway through that Ben Stiller movie *There's Something About Mary*. You know the one where Cameron Diaz plays a character we're all supposed to adore but I always thought was ditzy and annoying? So I wasn't too perturbed when Paul burst into the room, grabbed the remote control, and pressed the Pause button.

"We're engaged!" he said, holding Jan's ring finger up as evidence while she tittered and blushed beside him.

I remember drawing in breath and darting my eyes to my parents, expecting fireworks and not of the good kind, but that didn't happen. My mother jumped up and swept Jan into a hug, and my father pumped Paul's fist as though *he* was the lucky bastard who'd just scored Cameron Diaz!

Paul was nineteen. Jan his first and only girlfriend. How could they want that for him? How could anyone? I was young, but even then I suspected he was giving up so much. Unlike our rebellious older brother, Paul hadn't done anything remotely interesting, and now he was about to get *married*? I was overwhelmed with sadness. But I was brought up properly, so I feigned delight and jumped up and offered my own hugs.

It was only later, after the happy couple had dashed off to the share the news down at the local pub, that I asked Mum about it. I fully expected the mask to drop and the truth to come out. I expected words like "too young" and "wild oats" and "we have to put a stop to this nonsense!"

Except she was even more gushing. "Oh it's so wonderful, so fantastic! I couldn't be happier!" And she actually sounded sincere.

"But Jan's so *boring*," I wailed. "And... and I thought he'd travel and stuff."

"They can still *travel*, darling, they're not getting locked up." She laughed, and then her smile straightened a little and she added, "Jan may seem boring to you, darling, but she'll be *good* for Paul; she'll take care of him. And that's what Paul needs. She's perfect."

Really? I understood the sentiment, but wasn't it *Peter* who needed a caretaker not the boring middle brother? Paul didn't look like he'd ever get up to any kind of mischief. He was already good. He was better than good; he was as boring as Jan.

I didn't understand any of it at the time, but over the years, as I heard stories of Paul losing his wallet and locking his keys in the car and being useless with the household budget and the washing and cooking, all told with peals of laughter from the "better half," I started to comprehend.

Paul didn't score himself a bride so much as a babysitter. It wasn't that he'd found the perfect match. He'd just found someone willing and able to run his life and, failing that, rescue him when required. And I don't know why that irked me so much because, as I said before, I could see the value in a babysitter, at least I could for Peter.

So why couldn't I be happy for them?

It seems to me there are two types of people in this world—those who wave their hands in rough seas and those who dive in to save them. I know it's hard to picture now, but I used to be the latter.

It's the reason I rescued stray animals and took a job as a personal assistant and stayed friends with Tessa despite everything. I know my mother likes to repeat that story of her rescuing me at the age of four, but the truth is I rescued her right back. I know it's a corny line from another Hollywood flick, but I paid my dues over and over with Tessa. She wasn't the most popular girl in school, but I stuck by her side. She went through a bulimic phase, but I pulled her through, sticking to her like glue until I knew every meal had been properly digested (that's a lot of loitering outside toilet cubicles, folks!). When her dad cleared out, I practically moved into her bedroom until she could get through the night without bawling. I did the same when her first love tore her heart to shreds and when she didn't get the university entrance score she was expecting and when she got fired from that crappy job she couldn't stand but which still seemed to cut her like a knife.

Tessa was always the more vulnerable of the two of us, and I know now that's why my mother would tell that silly little story of Tessa pulling me out from behind the paint stand. It was about boosting *Tessa's* self-esteem, not undermining mine. My mother was a rescuer too, and she rescued Tessa almost as often as I did (why else would she let me sleep at another girl's house so often?).

And I guess that's why Mum welcomed Jan into our life, because now she wouldn't need to look out for Paul quite so much. At least one son had his own lifeguard. Pity about the other.

But all this has got me thinking, and no doubt you're wondering the same thing. When did I switch from the lifeguard to the one madly waving? When did I morph back into the girl behind the easel? When did I become so needy that so many people just assumed I'd put a gun to my head and pull the trigger?

I think about my job now. The one I lost six months ago. Was *that* the catalyst?

I've been avoiding this subject—I know I have—but perhaps it's time to 'fess up. I told you I was a PA and that I really loved the role, so why did I leave? Why did I do that?

Because, dear reader, twelve months before that, I began to let the balls drop.

It all started with a missing client file—I still can't imagine where I filed it—that was punctuated with several smashed cups and occasional sobbing sessions in the ladies bathroom, and it ended with my resignation, which I'm mortified to say was accepted hastily with a bottle of warm champagne and a Good Luck! card that was inked with relief.

I was no longer the rescuer, and no one seemed very willing to rescue me back.

CHAPTER 16

Okay, enough of the pity party. I think we're getting sidetracked. I can feel the energy rising in Dad's study, and I am sensing it's important. Louise is pointing to something on her laptop, and Ruth is shaking her head in wonder. No, that's not wonder. That's disbelief and regret. She's beating herself up.

"I *knew* he sounded familiar," she says. "Dammit. I should have gone with my gut."

"What?" says Craig, glancing at the screen over her shoulder. He, too, reads for a bit before his eyes widen.

"Whoa," he says. "Okay, that explains the drugs then. He's got form! Is that *two* deaths he's been linked to?"

Ruth is still shaking her head. "And here he is, showing up at another. I can't believe he didn't mention this earlier tonight. Like we couldn't have looked it up."

"You think he brought the drugs?" says Kelly, and Craig is nodding for her.

"'Course he did, who else? And he thought we'd never find them!"

You nearly didn't, you idiots. If it wasn't for the SOCOs, that packet would still be bobbing up and down with every flush. I have no idea who they're talking about, but it's got me excited. Whoever it is, he's clearly a criminal and it's clearly not my brother.

Ruth turns to Craig. "Please tell me you got his contact details. His *real* details, that is."

Craig pulls out his notebook and begins madly flicking through it while my heart begins to thump wildly. I watch for a few moments as he turns back a few pages then lets out a yelp and starts jabbing a number into his phone.

"I've got him!" he says, but my focus is suddenly shifting again.

I have another memory flash, but this one is very fresh and I just know it has to be related.

I am standing on the pool deck, staring at my phone while Justin Bieber massacres the Spanish language and someone screeches with laughter from the daybed. Then another sound catches my attention. It's coming from inside the house, and it does not feel right. I frown. I step inside, and that's when I see it, a tall silhouette of a man at the front of the house.

He has something at his side. What is that? He looks annoyed, no, aggravated. I feel a prickle of alarm. I want to ask what he's doing there, but there's something in his eyes that shuts me up.

I've seen the man before. I know him. I am suddenly awash with panic.

And now Craig and Kelly are rushing down my hallway and through my house. They reach the front door and burst through it and then down the driveway.

I watch with fascination as they make a beeline for the street, striding, one after the other, in the direction of Tessa's place. From this angle it looks like they've got dibs on who'll reach the house first.

Kelly wins the prize and throws himself at the front doorbell.

It buzzes loudly, quickly followed by a series of blunt knocks that reverberate through the hallway like a jackhammer. Mrs McGee starts at the sounds but Una is already up and opening it, her eyes widening, too, when she sees Kelly standing on her doorstep, Craig close behind.

"Is Vijay Singh on the premises?" Kelly asks, almost

breathless from his sprint over.

She nods blankly, half turns, but Vijay is already there, his keys in his hand, his vest now buttoned up. It is as though he has been waiting for this all night. He looks defiant, almost smug.

"Hello, officers," he says, sounding far too cheerful considering their presence.

"Detective Sergeant Powell would like us to escort you back to the May house for some more questions," Kelly says.

He nods, not asking why.

"What's going on?" This is Tessa, entering the hallway with Roco, cigarettes still alight.

Then Arabella steps forward, her eyes frantic. "But... but Vijay, honey, will you be coming back?"

He doesn't answer her, but that term of endearment answers an earlier question, don't you think? Now we know who was hooking up in the spare bedroom. Although you probably already worked it out. Your brain's in better shape than mine.

Vijay turns to Kelly and says, "Give me a moment."

Then he steps away from the officers, but it's Una he grabs on to, not Arabella, first holding her by both hands, then dragging her into his embrace.

"It's okay," he says. "It's going to be okay. I'm innocent. You have to remember that."

Then he hugs her even tighter, and it makes her whole body stiffen, but it's not his touch that's upsetting her. He's whispering something in her ear, something like "not now" and "incriminating," but the police don't catch that.

Kelly just looks impatient and starts to wave a hand in the air as if to say "Yeah, yeah, no time for schmaltz."

Vijay releases Una, then steps back and turns around to follow the officers out, only stopping halfway down the driveway to yell back, "Go back to the family, Una! Go back!"

Arabella looks confused, even a little put out, but Tessa is mortified and is staring daggers at Una.

"What's he on about?" she demands. "What does he mean, he's 'innocent'? He's not a *client* at your law firm, is he, Una? Tell me you didn't bring a *criminal* to Maisie's party!" Then, an eyebrow pitched high, she adds, "And what did he just give you?"

Aha! So Tessa saw that too. Did you?

When he hugged her tight, Vijay slipped something flat and pink into Una's jacket pocket. It has to be that pilfered envelope.

Una blinks down at Tessa as if she, too, is confused, then reaches into her pocket and retrieves the pink envelope, staring at it as though it's a white rabbit.

She looks back at Tessa again, her expression now one of alarm as the others start crowding in.

"Yeah, what was that about?" This is Leslie, Jonas just behind her, Roco close by.

Arabella has stepped back, however, and is holding one ear, the one without the earring. She is thinking *What a bastard.*

Now it's Una's turn to step away, but she doesn't look angry or smug or defiant. She looks panic-stricken and shoves the envelope back into her pocket.

"It's nothing," she says. "Nothing at all."

"Come on, what does he mean he's innocent?" Tessa persists. "Why wouldn't he be innocent? What the hell is going on?"

"I don't know. I don't know!" Una is in a flap, and Tessa's eyes are firing up.

Arabella has now dropped onto the couch while Mrs McGee is clutching the kitchen door as though it's the only thing keeping her up.

"You brought that man to the party, Una!" Tessa's voice is rising, her pitch getting hysterical. "Who the hell is he? What did he *do*?"

Una's palms are out. "I don't know... I didn't..."

103

She backs up towards Arabella, then drops down beside her and crumples.

Oh, Maisie, Una thinks to me. *Oh honey, I didn't think… Honest, I didn't. I'm so sorry…*

Everybody is staring at her, aghast, including me, and when she looks up, she recoils before swallowing stiffly.

"I need to tell you guys something," she says.

Then the sound is suddenly switched off.

Oh no you don't! *No, no, no, no, no!* Don't you dare hide from me, Una Conway! You turn the volume back up this instant!

But Una's now whispering furtively to the group, and most of them are looking shocked and alarmed except for Arabella, who just looks embarrassed.

Dammit, Una, what did you *do*? Or, more importantly, *what have you been up to?*

Because it's too late for silence, and I think I know your secret.

I'm not sure what Vijay's story is—I can't get my head around that yet—but I do know one thing for sure. I saw that pink envelope, Una, and this time I saw it clearly. It had the initials DM scribbled in Biro across the front and, below that, a clumsily drawn love heart.

Are you keeping up, dear reader? Do you understand what I'm saying?

Those are my *father's* initials—David May—and the handwriting… Oh God, the handwriting is not my mother's.

CHAPTER 17

"It's all your fault." This is the ugly dead guy, Neal, and he's by my side again.

I swing around to stare at him. "What? *Why*?"

"You're not ready to hear it yet. You're not ready to face the truth."

I am! I am! I am! I am!

"Then why is that conversation still hidden from you?"

"I don't know!" I screech back at him. Honestly I don't.

I glance back down to Una, who despite having everyone's rapt attention, looks absolutely bleak, guilty too. Do you think she looks guilty?

I wish I could see into her jacket, into those large, lumpy pockets and double-check that envelope. The writing was not my mother's, but it was deeply familiar. It can't be Vijay's, I know that much, so it must be Una's; it just has to be. Nothing else fits.

Is *that* what she was doing in my father's study earlier tonight? Was she penning him a letter and, if so, why?

Why would a work friend be leaving my father a letter on blush-coloured stationery with love hearts? Why would she have his personal mobile number for that matter? A mobile he never told me about? A number I was never given.

I told you Una had dangerous taste in men. Did I also tell you she liked them older and married if she could manage it? But it was worse than that. She was unapologetic about it.

"Single men are so needy," she told me once, "at least young men are. That's why I go for older blokes, the attached ones."

The two needn't necessarily be linked, I wanted to tell her; there are plenty of *single* older men who'd be happy to treat you like crap.

"Older married men are more blasé," she continued. "They keep it light; there's no strings attached."

"Well, apart from the wives' apron strings of course," I ventured, unable to help myself. It was one thing to joke about this, but these were real people's lives, I remembered thinking. Am thinking now, but she scoffed as if it was inconsequential.

Then she mocked me and said, "You're so old-fashioned, Maisie, honey, you *really* are."

Like affairs are a harmless twenty-first-century invention.

I shake the thought away irritably and try to think more recently. Did she flirt with Dad? Did he flirt back? *Of course* he flirted back; he flirts with all my friends.

Did she read that incorrectly, or was there something more serious going on?

My heart drops again. I taste bile in my mouth.

Surely my dad and Una weren't... Urgh, I can't even say the words out loud, and if you're thinking what I'm trying not to think, you can scrub your mind out with soap.

There is no way that Dad... There is no way that Una...

And what has *any* of this got to do with my murder?
Think, Maisie, think!

Did I go back and read that letter? Did I confront Una about it? She's a big girl; we all know who'd come out second best if things turned violent.

Neal snorts beside me, and I turn to catch him mid-eye roll. He's as bad as Kelly. It makes me want to scream.

"What?" I say to him. "You think I'm overreaching?"

"I think you're getting distracted again." Then he nods his head towards my house and repeats the words Vijay uttered just recently. "Go back to the family, Maisie. Go back."

And so I tear my eyes away from that silent confessional and back towards my house, noticing as I do so that several sets of neighbours are still awake. One man is peeking through the blinds, as though waiting for an encore, others lie under blankets, shifting and turning and shifting again, pummelling pillows like they wish it was my face. They're annoyed with me now, angry that my death has interrupted their slumber, and unlike Una, they don't care if I know it.

Well excuse me for keeping you up! I want to bellow. *How dreadfully rude and inconvenient of me!*

I feel like haunting them now. I feel like whooshing down and rattling the bedcovers, but that very thought has Neal tut-tutting.

"I'm not going to do it," I tell him.

"Tempting though, isn't it? When I died, the old farts across the road threw a party. And I'm not talking the sobbing to the tunes of Nick Drake type of party that your mates are throwing. I mean, Flora and Lionel Johnson were thanking the Lord that the likes of me were no longer walking the earth and corrupting others."

"Horrible," I say.

"Typical," is his response. "I really wanted to punish them. I had great plans. Was going to make their old video tape of *The Wizard of Oz* levitate." He giggles. "Deseree stopped me. Party pooper." He smiles. "But enough about me. We're getting sidetracked again." Then he brings a broken finger to his lips and makes a shushing sound. "It's not over yet, Maisie, not by a long shot."

Sniggering, he adds, "Sorry, I just know how much you

love a good pun!" before floating back to the tunnel.

Now it's my turn to roll my eyes, but I do as he suggests and focus back on the detectives. Ruth is sitting across from Vijay at the kitchen table, as though waiting for the entrée to be served up. Craig stands behind Vijay. Kelly behind Ruth. Tanner has long gone, which is just as well, and Louise is in the study trawling through Dad's emails.

No one is speaking, but Vijay doesn't look quite so smug now.

Ruth takes a deep breath, then recites Vijay's legal rights while he nods along, almost melodically, as though it's a tune he's heard many times before.

"Now, I'd like to ask you about Anya Mirakai and Geraldine Smythe." He stares at her and says nothing, so she adds, "I'd like to ask you about their suspicious deaths."

His lips droop a little. "I can't see why. I was acquitted on both counts. And I'm pretty sure the report you've just been looking at tells you that."

She licks her lower lip. "Your fingerprints were discovered at the homes of both women; they found some correspondence between you and Mrs Smythe."

He shrugs. "So we chatted. I made a few visits. She was a sad old dear. I was just keeping her company. That's not a crime, detective."

"It is if you killed her."

"And yet I didn't." He meets her eyes and does not flinch. "You do understand the meaning of the word 'acquitted,' yes, Detective?"

She smirks and thinks, *Smug bastard,* then says almost as an afterthought, "Did you have anything to do with the death of Maisie Leanne May?"

He leans back in his seat, forcing the chair onto two legs.

My mother hated the way my brothers used to do that.

Would admonish them every single time. *"You'll break the chair,"* she'd say. *"You'll break your back."*

I hope he leans out further.

Ruth repeats the question, and now Vijay looks disappointed in her.

He says, "I'd like to see my lawyer now."

And Ruth just nods, clearly expecting this, but I am furious. That wasn't an answer. He didn't refute anything. Is Tessa right? Did Una inadvertently bring a cold-blooded killer to my party? It's all so outlandish I can hardly think.

Luckily, Ruth is doing the thinking for me. She packs him off in a patrol car headed for police headquarters where she'll join him later for an official interrogation, his lawyer by his side, no doubt.

Vijay seemed neither alarmed by this development nor surprised, but I am suddenly feeling quite deflated. Is that *all* this is? A random killing by a friend of a friend, a crazy client of Una's? Was I just in the wrong place at the wrong time?

Please, Death, don't make it as depressingly shallow as that!

It's such an anticlimax.

I turn away. I make my way to the tunnel. I'm ready to hold up the white flag.

Deseree is standing there now, Emie by her side, Neal nowhere to be seen. Good. I'm fed up with his Royal Smugness.

"Okay," I tell them. "I'm done. Let's get this over with."

"But it's not over," says Deseree, and I snort.

"Well, it's over for me. I don't think I care anymore. So Vijay killed me because he's a psychopath, or maybe it has something to do with Una, I don't know. Makes no difference, really. I'm worm fodder no matter how it pans out. The party's over now, anyway, might as well mosey on over to the tunnel and get on with it."

Deseree is shaking her head. "I told you before. It doesn't work like that."

"Well, it does for me! You tell... *whoever* it is back there calling the shots, you tell them that I'm ready. I'm good to go! Let's fire up the engines, people, let's get this show on the road!"

They both just look at me sadly. Their sympathy is worse than Neal's smugness.

I groan. "*Why?*" I sound like my toddler self again.

"Read Rule #4 again," Deseree says as the tunnel swallows her and Emie away.

Rule 4. Thou shall see all when thou is open to seeing.

Hello! I'm open! I'm here, aren't I? I'm trying!

I stare after the vanishing light and scowl, then back towards earth where Craig is also scowling. He's flicking through his notepad frantically, his eyebrows wedged together.

No, dammit, no, he is thinking. *It just doesn't work.*

I don't know what he's looking for or what doesn't add up, but I don't care anymore, and it's not because I'm over all this. It's because I can hear a very familiar sound, and it makes my heart break.

The two people I love most in this world have arrived home, and I'm stuck here to witness their misery.

Thanks, Deseree, thanks a lot.

CHAPTER 18

A dusty silver station wagon is just pulling into our street, rattling down the road and sliding into position at the bottom of our driveway. It's my folks, of course, and they are not in any hurry.

The engine is switched off, but for several minutes neither of them gets out. They just sit there staring at the road ahead, and at first I am offended. Why aren't they rushing in, all guns blazing?

And then it makes sense. I get it now. By opening their car doors, they will beckon in a new reality, a darker dawn, so they're putting it off. They're procrastinating. That's all very well, guys, but you're already six hours late.

I think it's time.

Eventually, slowly, my mum's door creaks open. Followed a beat later by my dad's. I see one leg, then another, then two more. I see them shuffle onto the sidewalk and reach for each other. I see them take a deep breath before turning to stare up at the front door, their eyes wary, as if approaching a haunted house. Which I guess, if you think about it, it is.

I wonder, too, if they intend to knock, but I never get to find out. The door has swung open, and Detective Ruth stands there, a grim look on her face.

She beckons them in as though she's the butler, then shakes both their hands and leads them down the hallway, away from the office where my blood is still splattered and

111

towards the kitchen, where I can hear the kettle boiling.

The sound seems too parochial, considering the circumstances.

My parents follow Ruth, as though strangers in their own home. Has my death ruined everything now? Has it turned our home back into a house, albeit a creepy one, one that not even slick rendering or lush vines can combat?

"I'm sorry for your loss," Ruth says, pointing them into their own kitchen chairs.

They blink at her. My mother nods. They dutifully sit down.

"Kelly will make us a cup of tea." She flashes a glance at her sidekick, who doesn't exactly look thrilled by this. He thinks the task is below him and is wondering why Craig can't do it. "Do you mind my asking you a few questions now? Or would you rather—"

"Now," my mother says loudly. Then more softly she adds, "Now is fine."

Ruth nods and takes the chair across from them, placing her hands prayer-like on the table. She breathes in, waits a few seconds, then exhales.

"Can you tell me when you last saw your daughter?"

"Two days ago," starts Dad, but Mum interrupts.

"It was Thursday, just before eleven. We had packed the car for the drive. She was in my sewing room, reading a magazine. We both went in to say goodbye."

"She didn't come out to see you off?"

My mother stares at her, frowning. "She... no. No she didn't."

"And what state of mind was she in? Could you tell?"

"She was *fine*." This is Dad, and he is determined to speak. He is determined to let this woman know that I was in perfectly good spirits, thanks very much for asking.

And yet even I am having trouble believing that.

I was holed up inside at eleven a.m. on a weekday, for goodness' sake. I couldn't even find the enthusiasm to see my parents off. Not so fine perhaps.

"She hasn't been great," says Mum, ignoring his outburst. No, it is *because* of his outburst. She is addressing this to him, and he is glaring at the tabletop like he finds the cheap pine offensive. "She had to leave her job, you see, and she really loved that job. And she broke up with Roco—"

"He's a ratbag!"

My mother waits a beat. "They broke up *amicably*, David." She smiles pointedly at the detective. "As I told you on the phone, she was struggling with it all. She was not great."

My father closes his eyes as though that will somehow block out what she is saying.

"She was depressed?" Ruth asks, and Mum's eyes flicker with impatience.

"Wouldn't you be?" Now she sounds defensive.

Ruth nods, but she doesn't look convinced. Perhaps she doesn't love her job as much as I did. Perhaps she doesn't have a Roco in her life.

"Have either of you ever met or had any interactions with a man named Vijay Singh. Dr Vijay Singh."

They both stare at her, baffled by the change of tack.

Eventually Mum says, "No. Why? Who is he?"

"He attended your daughter's party, Mrs May. That's all I can say at this stage of the investigation."

I expect her to object to that, to demand some answers, but she drops it immediately and just smiles at Kelly as he hands her a teacup.

"Milk? Sugar?" he asks, and Mum goes to get up, but he waves her back down. "I'm sure I can manage."

Mum smiles again, grateful, then she turns her eyes back to Ruth and her face seems to fall into itself. Her shoulders drop. She is no longer smiling.

"Do you know…" She falters, closes her own eyes for a moment, then opens them and says more assuredly, "Can you tell me what happened, please?"

Ruth looks puzzled by the question and waits as Kelly places milk and sugar on the table and then hands my father his cup.

"Your daughter died from a fatal gunshot to the head, Mrs May. I did explain that over the phone."

"Yes, yes." Mum sounds impatient again. This is not what she's asking. "I just want to know, do you know *for a fact* that she...?"

Mum can't quite bring herself to say it, and I see Dad shrink into himself and reach for his cup. He wishes it was whisky.

Ruth says gently, "We can't rule out suicide, Mrs May, not at this stage. But we are keeping an open mind. We're looking at all avenues."

"All avenues?" This is Dad now, glancing up from his brew. He looks buoyed suddenly.

"It's early days, Mr May, but we have found some evidence that others may be involved."

"This man you mention? This doctor?"

"Perhaps." Yet for some reason she doesn't look convinced. "I need to ask about the gun."

Dad's shoulders fall again, his gaze dropping back to his cup while Mum's eyes slide his way. Does she blame him, I wonder?

Ruth says, "You stored the gun on two hooks in your office, is that correct Mr May?"

He swallows. "Yes, but... but it was an old piece of junk. I didn't even know it still *worked*."

"Why wouldn't it *work*, David?" says Mum, her voice rising in pitch.

Yep, definitely blames Dad.

"Because it's a million years old, *Mandy*," he says through clenched teeth. "It wasn't even loaded. How was I to know?"

"Because it's a *gun*, David, an actual working gun. Not something you found at Toys R Us. You understand that, right?"

Ruth holds a placatory palm up. She needs to get this back on track, she needs to keep this couple calm; they're no use to her if they're arguing. "And you say it wasn't loaded, Mr May? Where were the bullets stored?"

Dad looks from Mum to her, his frown easing. "In one of the drawers in my desk, the bottom one, right at the back, I can assure you of that. I never showed anyone. I certainly never showed Maisie."

Ruth nods. She emits a sigh. "I know this is confronting, but I need you to take a look in your office for me, Mr May. I need to ascertain if anything has been disturbed, if anything is missing."

He looks confused again, but Mum has rallied and is already on her feet.

"Good," she says. "Of course." Then, noticing Dad still sitting there hunched over his cup, she almost snaps, "Come on then, David. This is no time for tea. Let's face the music, shall we?"

Wow, she really does blame Dad, doesn't she? The incrimination in her voice is agonising to hear, yet I wonder if it's the only thing keeping her from falling apart. Blame can be quite motivating, almost energising when you think about it.

In contrast, guilt is clearly crippling, and I watch as Dad pushes his cup away and struggles to his feet. He suddenly looks all of his seventy-four years. Louise goes to help him, but he shakes her away, then follows Ruth down the hallway towards ground zero.

At the office doorway, Ruth stops and says, "No further, please."

But Dad is not listening. The walk has reenergised him, and he is already pushing past her and inside. Ruth goes to grab his arm, but it is too late. He is staring at the carpet to the side of his desk. He is staring at the remnants of me, the smattering of blood I left behind. He stiffens, he chokes, he drops to his knees and he breaks into gulping sobs.

And now I am sobbing right beside him.

I wish I could reach out. I wish I could hug him, but I'm also surprised because I thought Dad would be the stoic, dry-eyed one and Mum would be the one who turned to jelly. I mean, she was always good in a crisis, but she was my *mother*! How can she be so together? How can she still be upright?

I guess it all comes back to that gun.

After a few agonising minutes, Mum's demeanour softens and I am relieved to see her step towards Dad, lean down a little, and gently start patting his back, like she's soothing a naughty child. Ruth shoots worried glances between them, but she's not thinking about the warring couple. She's thinking they mustn't go any further. She must preserve the integrity of the crime scene.

Oh my baby girl, I can hear Dad think now, and it sets me off again. *If only you hadn't gone on that bloody date.*

I do a double take and swallow back my sob. *Sorry, what?*

If only that night with Jonas had never happened.

Hang on, is he talking about my date with Hottie Hodder? Is *that* what's upsetting him? Not the fact that he brought a gun into our home or hung it on the wall or left the bullets lying around for any nutter to uncover but the fact that I went to an Italian restaurant one chilly winter's night with Jonas?

What does a harmless date with a good-looking guy have to do with my murder?

Now I feel more muddled up than ever.

CHAPTER 19

As Mum continues to soothe Dad, I try to get my head straight. I try to work out why my father's first thought when he saw that blood was of Jonas. As was Tessa's, now that I think about it.

Perhaps I haven't looked at Jonas closely enough. He *was* the first to find my body, and the way Roco and Tessa were just talking, well, I have to ask: Is there more to Jonas than meets the eye? Does he have something to do with this?

I try to think back...

Jonas wasn't nicknamed Hottie Hodder for nothing. He was the best looking guy in my social circle, a work friend of Tessa's and, at least until recently, Roco's best mate. When it comes to friendship, Roco is a serial monogamist, and his latest bromance was with Jonas, a man who could down a schooner of beer in seconds, banter about football for hours and always be relied upon for a good time. He's what Aussie guys call a "top bloke."

To the women, however, it was all about the body. Jonas wasn't tall and dark so much as fit and blond—Ryan Gosling and Bradley Cooper rolled into one with the six-pack to match. Yet when he asked me out on a date that winter, I had to smile and let him down.

"You know Tessa's got a major crush on you, right?"

He smiled back. He shrugged nonchalantly. He said,

"So? What's that got to do with us?"

"She's my *friend*, Jonas. She's *your* friend too. It's how we met! I couldn't do that to her."

"That's the problem, yeah? Tessa has monopolised us both."

"What are you talking about?"

"She's always around. Like a bad smell. This has got nothing to do with Tessa. I just want to get to know *you* better. Get some quality time with the amazing Ms May."

I was flattered. I can't say I wasn't, but I was also surprised, and I asked him why he assumed I was so amazing.

"You're just so... together." I looked at him, puzzled, and he laughed. "I mean, you're beautiful and you have a great job and friends, and well, you just have your shit together, that's all. Unlike most of the chicks around here. Unlike bloody Tessa." He laughed again. "You're the whole package, Maisie. Tessa's not. Why should you be punished because your best mate has a crush that's going nowhere?"

Now it was my turn to laugh. "Oh, I see. So not going out with you would be a form of punishment, is that what you're saying?"

He smiled his silky smile. "I guess you'll have to accept my invitation and find out for yourself."

And still I resisted. "I'm just not sure I can do it to Tess."

"Why not?" His smile had vanished. "She'd do it to you."

"No she wouldn't," I snapped back. I knew that for a fact. Or at least I thought I did.

Then he smiled at me again. It was the full Hollywood throttle—the gleaming white teeth, the tilt of the head, the slight squint of the eyes. "It's just dinner, Maisie. I'm not asking you to get married."

He made a good point.

"I didn't think you even liked Jonas," said Tessa when I

fessed up later that day. I had to tell her—of course I did—but I cushioned the blow by explaining that it was just a quick pizza down at Bill and Tony's Ristorante.

"Nothing's going to happen, Tess. He'll work out I'm dull as dishwater and quickly lose interest."

She gave me a strange look then. "You're worried about me," she said.

"No, I'm not."

"I'm not into him anymore, is that what you think?" She laughed. She sounded genuine. Then her laughter stopped. "Just be careful there, okay? He's not as hot as he seems."

"What does that mean?"

"Nothing. Now I'm just being a bitch. Go out, have fun, be free!"

I think about her comments now. Was that why she decided Roco was fair game? Because, in girlfriend land at least, I'd already crossed the line? I had lost her loyalty.

But I digress. I don't think it's the date with Jonas that Dad is referring to now. I know he was happy to see me step out of my comfort zone and "let my hair down." I'd been single for some time and a bit down in the dumps. No, I think Dad is referring to the *end* of that date, the bit where it all went to hell in a handbasket.

Despite my promises to Tessa, something did happen that night, something pretty momentous, although the date itself was relatively benign.

We talked, we flirted a little, we even squabbled at one point—he thought the #MeToo movement was pathetic; I thought it was a powerful concept. But we put our differences aside when the food arrived. We were in too good a mood to argue.

We shared a delicious pumpkin-and-goat-cheese pizza, Jonas and I, washed down with plenty of good Shiraz. So much wine, in fact, that few people were surprised when I went hurtling down the restaurant stairs on my way out and broke my leg.

Few people that is, except Jonas. He was horrified.

The day after I was released from hospital, my leg in a cast, my head pounding like a jackhammer—I guess I must have hit the wall on the way down, it all happened so fast—he backed right off. Suddenly he didn't want to upset Tessa. They were colleagues; it could prove uncomfortable at work.

I saw Jonas after that from time to time—hanging out with the gang, at parties, a few hours ago, in fact—and he was always friendly enough, but he could never quite look me in the eye, at least not for very long. It was though I had ruined the mirage.

I was the silly little drunk who fell flat on her face. The amazing Ms May had been vanquished.

Was that when I lost all sense of control? Did my self-confidence shatter right along with my right tibia? And does Dad blame *Jonas* for that? More importantly, did I confront Jonas about it all last night? Did I demand a belated apology for his rejection? And was murder the result? Or did Tessa finally confront me? Demand to know how I could date the man she liked? Is that why I'm dead?

Oh it's all so damn silly, so trivial, in fact.

So why did Dad bring it up? Why was that the first thing he thought of when he saw all that blood?

"Please take a moment, Mr May," Ruth is saying, her voice low, her tone patient. But the truth is she doesn't want him to take long. She has questions, a dozen questions, and she wants to get on with it. It's been a very long night. Hell, the morning is practically upon us.

Dad is shaking the tears off, struggling back to his feet, when he lifts a weather-beaten finger and says, "What's my chair doing over there?"

Good question! Finally they're thinking outside the box. Someone clearly pushed it over there so they could reach the gun. Yes, let's focus on that.

"You didn't put it there?" Ruth asks.

"Of course I bloody didn't! It's always behind my desk." His guilt is making him rude and defensive again.

"And the gun was on the wall, just above the chair? Resting in that case?"

Ruth knows the answer to that, so why bother asking? It's almost as though she's on Mum's side and is rubbing his face in it.

Dad nods, chokes, hangs his head again. It makes my heart break. Mum is frowning now, but she is not thinking along the same lines as Ruth. She's now so outside the box she's in fresh territory.

"But the hooks aren't very high, are they?" Mum says. "Why would you need the chair to get to the gun?"

And before any of us can even compute that question, she has another more intriguing one. "And why is the photo like that?"

We all follow her eyes to the filing cabinet to the side of Dad's desk where there's a silver picture frame sitting beside a dusty nautilus shell. The frame is facing the wall so we can't see what it contains.

For a moment my memory fails me, and I can't quite remember the contents. Was it their wedding photo? A certificate of some sort? Then it comes to me with a whoosh. That's right! It's a happy snap taken on the last holiday we ever had as a family. I already told you about that. It was my final year of school, the setting an island in Vanuatu. We were all there, including Jan and at least one of her kids. We were standing on a sundrenched beach, Mum and Dad grinning happily, Peter looking stoned, Paul caught midblink, one arm slung around Jan who is half-cut from the picture, as though even the photographer didn't feel she quite belonged.

And me? I'm right in the middle of the fold, my smile as wide as Mum's, my arms spread out as if to say "Here we are, world, aren't we terrific!"

It's my favourite photo, so why is it facing away?

Mum attempts to retrieve it, but Ruth has a hand up.

"Allow me."

She steps carefully across the perimeter of the office, pulling a latex glove on as she does so. When she reaches the frame, she stops and turns back.

"I gather it doesn't normally face this way?"

"Of course not!" This is Dad again. He is as flabbergasted as my mother. "It's a picture of the whole family, our favourite one. Why would I have it facing the damn wall?"

I watch with curiosity as Ruth scoops it up, glances at it and then frowns. She looks up at my folks and then back at the frame, her frown deepening. Why is she frowning? I feel something slither down my back.

Slowly, almost gingerly, she makes her way to the door. When she reaches Mum, she shoots her an inscrutable look, then turns the frame to face my folks, and only then do I see what all the fuss is about.

It may have been our favourite family photo, but the frame is now empty.

CHAPTER 20

I suppose my parents gasp. I know I do, but Ruth is looking animated. Another clue! Another culprit, perhaps.

"Who would take…?" My mother starts. Stops.

"I'll kill 'em!" That's my dad. Livid.

I can't get my head around it. *Was it taken as a memento? Some kind of ghoulish souvenir?*

"I gather it was still in the frame before you left for Dubbo?" Ruth asks, and Dad rails again.

"Of course it bloody was!"

He's really got to get his temper under control. He's just lucky Ruth isn't taking it personally.

"As far as we recall," Mum adds more gently. "We can't say for sure, can we David? We've all been rather distracted of late. Maybe somebody took it earlier? Maybe Peter took it so he would have a picture of us to take back to London."

Dad scoffs at that, he does not agree, while I'm surprised once again by her clear thinking. Yet I too don't agree. Instead, my head is reeling and I'm almost as excited as Ruth. This has to be another clue! There's no other explanation. And it has to lead straight to the culprit. I don't know whether they took the picture before I was killed or after, but if we find the photo, I just know we'll find the killer.

Has anyone thought to frisk Vijay and see if he has it?

"Where are my boys? Are they still here?" This is Mum,

and she finally sounds fraught, like the picture has just reminded her that she has other children, that it's not all about me.

"One son was out by the pool earlier," Ruth tells her, signalling for Kelly, who has been loitering out in the hallway. "I'm not sure about the other. We had to keep them out of this area. The crime scene officers are just finishing in the living room too, so that space is also out of bounds for now. I trust you understand."

Mum looks at Ruth as though she doesn't understand any of it, then glances at the empty frame one more time as Ruth hands it to Kelly, before sighing heavily and making her way towards the back of the house.

Dad watches her leave, then slowly follows.

When they reach the sliding door to the back deck, Mum glances around and does not see Paul at first. He's half-asleep on the daybed under the pergola, the black splotch on the ground by his feet. Paul's wife has vanished. She's getting about a lot tonight.

"Peter?" Mum calls out. "Honey, is that you?"

The splotch stirs, shimmers, moves towards her. Paul looks up with a start and does the same. And then my heart breaks all over again as I watch my family embrace each other, or at least my family and the black blob.

All four of them find their way back to the daybed and fall into it. I think about what was happening on that bed just a few hours earlier. It seems a lifetime ago now.

Mum wipes a hand across her wet cheeks. I can see her hand is shaking. At last her true colours are showing. At last she's acting like my mother.

"Do you know what happened?" she says eventually. "Did you boys see anything? Were you close?"

Paul shakes his head, looks away. "I wasn't here. I'm sorry, Mum."

The guilt in his eyes matches my dad's. Mum reaches a hand to his and squeezes it, then they both stare towards the blob. A conversation ensues. I'm not privy to it, but I get the idea because Mum is now shaking her head, vehemently, while her hands are now calm and steady.

She holds one up like a traffic warden. "You cannot blame yourself, Peter. I will *not* allow it. I will not!" Her voice is strong. Her tone determined. "Maisie lived her own life, and she had a good life, really she did. You weren't responsible for that, and you aren't responsible for her death."

Peter must start to say something because she holds both hands up now and almost snaps at him. "Enough, Peter! Enough!"

Dad says, "You weren't to know, boy, you weren't to know."

Then Mum reaches one hand towards the shadow, and when she speaks again her tone is tender. "You *need* to let it go, my darling. It was not your job to protect Maisie, and she would not blame you. I know she would not."

And then he must have let it go because the darkness slowly dissipates and my eldest brother shimmers into view. It's the first I've seen of him since my death, and it sends my heart into a tailspin again.

Peter looks like a derelict version of himself, nothing like my handsome, swarthy oldest brother. His unbuttoned dinner shirt is smudged and wrinkled, his slick hair now dishevelled, his complexion raw and ruddy. It's like he's gone from polished timber to distressed wood in just one night.

Why was he beating himself up so hard? And why was he hiding himself from me? I assumed it had something to do with drugs, but maybe I misunderstood.

"How's Gramps?" I hear Paul ask, and I want to know—now, desperately—so I try to let that go. I try to concentrate.

"Hanging on," says Dad, who looks like he's only just hanging on himself.

I wonder how they feel about that. About being by an

old man's bedside when they could have been home, saving their young daughter instead.

Is that mean-spirited of me? Does youth naturally take precedence? It's funny how we worship the young and rescue them first, as though they are somehow more worthy. Why not the elderly? The people who have put the most in?

I'm trying to remember why I didn't go to Dubbo this time to visit Gramps or the last time now that I think about it. I wasn't working. I had nothing on my schedule. It can't be because of my party; that was planned after my folks left the house.

Was I always a bad granddaughter? A selfish one?

"Does Gramps know about Maisie?" Paul asks, and Mum shakes her head.

He'll know soon enough, I think. No, I *know* this. And it has nothing to do with them phoning him tomorrow or the fact that he's ninety-five and in palliative care. I just know he isn't long of this earth. It's a feeling I get. I can almost sense his presence. He's not far off. It's like he's started on this journey but hasn't quite hit the road yet. Is still gathering his swag, pulling on his boots, checking for traffic.

I long for Gramps suddenly, like a yearning ache. I wish he were here to help me get through this. I'd rather him than Neal and Deseree and that poor, ravished girl. Or even Grandma if I'm being honest. I never really got to know Grandma May. She died fifteen years ago, before we started making regular trips back to Nevercloud. The only memories I have of her are fragrant ones—the waft of fresh roses and blueberry jam and cinnamon. Lots and lots of cinnamon.

"She's a bloody good cook your gran."

That's Neal by my side again, but I am surprised by the comment, not his presence.

"You *know* my grandma? My actual grandmother?"

"Grandma Pickles and Pie? Of course! She makes a

mean pumpkin scone too. To die for." He sniggers at the pun, then rolls his eyes at my gaping mouth. "Everyone knows everyone; it's not that big a deal, honey."

"But how? There must be so many of you back there."

"Not really. We're just one cosmic force. It's hard to explain. You'll get it when you cross."

"And when will that be? How long have I got?"

He shrugs. "How long's a piece of string?"

My mouth is grimacing now, and he chuckles again. "In your case as long as you need. You get special privileges."

"Really? Why?"

He smiles at me sadly. "Because of the way you died, honey. I can't believe you haven't at least grasped that bit yet. You need extra time to come to terms with it all."

There must be a lot of Americans hovering between life and death then, I think, recalling recent statistics I read on gun deaths in the US. But there's something else I want to know, something I recall.

"What did you mean when you said you needed to get your points up?"

"Sorry? You've lost me."

"Earlier, when I first met you. You said—"

"I was just being a bitch." He sighs. "It's pretty simple. Once you do cross over, you have to help others across, it's part of the program."

"Program? What program?"

He holds up a broken limb. "Now we're getting distracted again, and it just won't do. You might have all the time in the world, honey, but I've got people to see, places to go, scones to eat!" He winks at me. "Come on, let's get our skates on."

"What do you mean?" I ask. "What people? What places?"

He shakes his head and sighs dramatically. "Nope, no, this time I'm not biting. You need to focus, woman, focus on *whodunit*."

"I already know who did it. I told Deseree that I know. You're clearly not keeping up."

He looks at me sideways. "You do?"

"Yes, it's obviously that dodgy character Vijay. You heard what the cops said earlier. He was up on murder charges. And now that I think about it, it's starting to make sense. He must have swiped that photo as a grisly memento, just like he swiped the envelope."

Neal shrugs. "Oh Vijay's not so bad. He got acquitted, remember?"

"Yes, twice, so he says. Doesn't mean he didn't do it."

"No. No it doesn't."

My ears prick up. "So are you saying he did do it? That he was guilty of killing those women?"

He looks at me impatiently. "Yes, no, maybe, maybe not. Doesn't necessarily mean he's your man though. Not in this case."

"Why not? It's perfect! He's a killer. He was at the scene of the crime. Surely it has to be him, surely no one else in my group could do such a thing!"

"And yet you continue to suspect them," he says, his voice as smooth as ice. "Have you noticed the way you do that?"

"I'm trying to get it all straight in my head! I'm trying to work out who did this."

"Then keep going," he says. "It's closer to home than you think."

And again he vanishes like a rat into the night while I hover above with nothing to do but watch my loved ones implode.

I can see that Ruth is watching them too, biding her time. She has more questions for my parents, and she wants to get back to the station, but she knows the best time to get answers, *honest, candid* answers, is when the parties involved are wrung out. And my family is as wrung out as a wet dishcloth.

Louise has just shown Ruth something on Dad's computer, and it's set her into another tailspin. I didn't catch what it was, but she snatched an item from the top of his desk and made a beeline for the back deck.

After a few more minutes, she coughs discreetly and catches my parents' eyes.

"Can I have another word?" she mouths, glancing at my brothers before adding, "In private."

They look at each other with matching frowns and then slowly get to their feet, following her back inside while my brothers watch them go, their eyes wary.

My parents are headed for the kitchen again, and I am about to follow when Paul makes an interesting comment.

"You weren't here, Pete. Where did you go?"

Ooh, good question. Let's hang around for a bit.

Peter frowns at him. "What?"

"After the party. You vanished."

"Nah, mate. No I didn't."

"Yeah, mate, yeah you did." His tone is mocking and impatient. "Cops said they couldn't find you."

"Couldn't find you either, right?"

"That's because I've moved house, you dickhead. Didn't have my new address. What's your excuse?"

"Oh just piss off, Paul," Peter says, turning his back to him. "I don't answer to you."

This only infuriates my other brother. "Just bloody tell me! Why are you being so evasive? What were you doing? Pulling chicks again? Scoring a hit? What? Just tell me where you were!"

"Nowhere, I was nowhere!" Then he rubs a hand through his hair and says, "I was just... I was at Central Station. Okay? Happy?"

Paul looks mystified by this, his brow furrowing, and I don't blame him. I'm equally mystified. Why would my oldest brother be loitering miles away at a grotty train station after midnight? It's hardly his style.

"Central?" Paul persists. "What were you doing there?"

"Nothing! Turns out I was doing nothing, going nowhere fast, so just leave it be, okay? *Please*, just... just drop it."

And Paul does, releasing a low growl as he gets to his feet, but I don't want to drop it. I think it's a really excellent question, and I'd also like to know why the word *Nevercloud* is being repeated over and over, like a broken record, inside Peter's head.

What was my brother doing at Central Station at midnight, and why is he thinking about Dad's property at a time like this?

Back in the kitchen, my parents are seated at the breakfast table again, which will forever be an interrogation desk to me now, and Ruth has produced a white slip of paper. It's the boarding pass I spotted on Dad's desk earlier tonight.

What has that trip to Vanuatu got to do with anything?

"Can you tell me about this?" Ruth says, passing it straight to my dad.

I'm expecting him to laugh and say, "What of it?" but he does the opposite. He stares at the pass like it's poison, no, worse than that, like it's porn, his face riddled with what looks to me like guilt again, but this time it's laced with disgust. He darts a look at Mum, who sits stony-faced beside him.

"What... what about it?" Dad manages.

"You took a recent trip to Thailand, Mr May."

It's a statement, and I expect him to dispute it, but he does the opposite. He nods.

She says, "Can you tell me why you were there?"

What's she talking about? Dad hasn't been to Thailand. She must have mistaken Peter's name for Dad's. She must have her wires crossed.

Dad glances back at Mum, who is staring straight ahead, glaring at the aqua-blue splashback, a garish metallic glass that she never liked and Dad never got round to replacing.

He says, "I just needed a break, that's all."

A break? Dad? That makes me laugh. Dad never needed "a break" in his life. He wasn't the "R&R" kind. And if he did want some rest and recreation, he'd head straight to his favourite place on earth (yes, Nevercloud), not some tacky resort in Koh Samui or wherever the hell he went.

I wish I could see that pass more clearly. Dad's covering most of it with his big lumpy paw. Does it really say Thailand?

"You went for three days? Alone?" Ruth asks, flashing a glance at my mother, and now his guilt turns to what looks like panic. His face has drained of colour, and his eyelashes are batting madly.

While he sits there, looking skittish, I try to recall the last time Dad went anywhere alone for more than a few hours. It was to Dubbo, wasn't it? Yes, that's right, last month, something about the farm and crisis management. I remember feeling sorry for Dad and relieved at the same time. At least Mum and I had escaped that particular road trip. Now I'm wondering if that's when he snuck off to Thailand.

Then something even more disturbing smacks me in the head.

Someone else went to Thailand recently, Bangkok if I remember right. Someone with blond hair and legs up to her eyeballs. Somebody who flirts with older men, preferably the married kind. My stomach turns. My head pounds. My heart reaches out to my mother.

"And it was just a holiday was it, Mr May. Just recreation? No other reason for your—?"

"Boss! You're gonna wanna see this!" That's Kelly, the only one with the guts to interrupt Ruth Powell midinterrogation.

She turns her glare upon him.

"Sorry," he adds quickly. "It's important."

She looks back at my parents with a stiff smile. "We'll discuss this later."

Then she gets up and walks out of the kitchen while my dad visibly slumps and Mum continues staring at the splashback.

Ruth continues glaring at Kelly all the way from the kitchen to the living room, where I notice several SOCOs gathered around the couch. It's been pulled out from the wall, and someone is taking photos of something on the other side.

The flash is sharp and unsettling, but it wipes the glare off Ruth's face. Now she just looks curious.

"What's the story, JJ?" she says, striding across, and the tattooed SOCO looks up from her camera and then nods back to the carpet.

Ah, now I see it! Now I see what all the fuss is about.

There's a stash of hundred dollar bills splayed out between the couch and the wall. So that's where all that money got to!

CHAPTER 21

If my parents have any clue as to the origins of that money—$775 as it turns out—they're not letting on. I think Dad's hiding something, but I'm not sure he even knows what it is he's hiding. He looks as puzzled as I feel.

Ruth has returned to the kitchen, cash in hand (well, in an evidence bag, if you must know), and she's smacked it down on the table before them. It's all very dramatic, like a scene from *Law & Order*, but they both just blankly stare at the bag.

"We found this down behind the sofa, the one in your living room. Any idea what it was doing there?"

Now they look at her blankly.

"Did either of you put it there, for example?"

They shake their heads.

"Is this where you normally stash extra cash? Perhaps you're not into the usual hidey-holes like under the mattress or, I don't know, a bank?"

Again, they shake their heads.

"Do either of you have any idea who *might* have put it there? There's almost $780 in this bag. That's not loose change, folks. That's not a bit of coinage slipping down between the cushions. Would one of your children have put it there?"

Again, the shaking of the heads. Mum looks completely lost, but she's also lost her energy and can't seem to fathom enough to enquire further, although she's clearly curious. Dad looks like it's starting to ring a bell, maybe, kind of. Perhaps.

Ruth catches this and zeroes in on him. "Mr May? Talk to me."

He shrinks back. He shakes his head. It's a safer response.

Ruth groans with exasperation. She does not believe him, but she, too, is tired and is running out of time. She has a slippery suspect to interrogate back at headquarters not to mention fingerprints to check and toxicology results to demand...

"Aherm."

This is Craig, standing at the kitchen door. He has his notepad in his hand, and he looks fit to bursting. He's really loving this gig. I wonder if he'll ask for a permanent transfer from Tanner's team and if Ruth will accept.

She whips her head around, offering him the same glare she gave Kelly when he interrupted her, but Craig's getting braver. He holds firm, darting glances at his pad as if it's the Holy Grail.

Ruth groans even louder and turns back to my parents. "The SOCOs are finishing up now, Mr and Mrs May, and we'll all be out of your hair very soon," she begins, not surprised by the relief that washes across both their faces. "But don't think we won't be back. This isn't over, folks."

"Can I see my daughter?" Mum asks, and again, it feels as though it's only just occurred to her. "I need to see my baby." Her voice cracks.

This wipes the condescension from Ruth's tone. "Of course, Mrs May. I'll arrange that tomorrow." She glances towards the window. "Later this morning, I mean."

Mum nods, a tear dripping from one eye.

Ruth gives her a tight smile, then scoops the cash back up and leaves my parents sitting together in their kitchen. They've never looked more alone.

Again, I want to reach down. I want to wrap them in a ghostly embrace, but Ruth is already motioning for Craig to join her in the living room, and I am keen to learn what it is he's so confident about.

Only when they reach the room, only when they know they're out of earshot, does Ruth stop and turn to him, an eyebrow raised questioningly.

"Vijay Singh couldn't have done it, ma'am," Craig says, his tone elevated.

"And you know this, how?"

"I questioned everybody earlier. I have their alibis. Dr Singh was with one of the other guests in the spare bedroom, you know, doing stuff."

"*Doing stuff?* What are you, twelve?"

He blushes. "Having sexual relations, his words, not mine." He glances down at his pad. "During the pivotal hour and a half, Mr Singh and a woman called Arabella Simpson were first at the pool, then in the kitchen, then in the guest bedroom, the one upstairs. Several witnesses have confirmed it. His presence is accounted for."

"They could be in it together," she says, and he shrugs.

"Mutual friends insist they only met each other last night."

She frowns, thinks about that and then winces. "And you're only just telling me *now?* Now that we've hauled him down to headquarters and dragged his cranky solicitor out of bed!"

"Sorry, ma'am, but I thought you'd want me to check, to be certain."

"And you are certain?"

"Yes, I am. I just phoned the woman in question, Ms Simpson. She confirms that she only met Dr Singh this evening and was with him from about eleven until the victim was discovered around twelve fifteen. The pathologist says Maisie was probably shot between eleven thirty and midnight, so…" He lets her do the math.

"She doesn't sound happy, ma'am, this Arabella Simpson. In fact, she asked if you could pass a message along to Mr Singh."

"Really? And what message is that?"

"She said to tell him to, um…" He blushes again. "To, er, go f-word himself."

Ruth stifles a smile, and I can't help giggling. We both agree that sounds like the genuine sentiments of a woman who's just been used and spat out, not an accomplice providing a fake alibi.

"Sorry, ma'am, but I think he's in the clear."

"Yeah," she says, "more's the pity."

And, again, I agree. The sleazy doctor was such a good suspect! So remote and detached from my life, I was happy to pin it on him. Now we're back to square one.

Now we're back to my loved ones.

CHAPTER 22

The sun is just peeping up from behind Tessa's house, lending it a rosy glow. It looks shiny and new. There's a sparkle coming from one of the top windows, and the low lighting has muted the patchy paintwork. It seems as though someone's just given it a bath and popped on some fresh lippie.

Must be a trick of the light. That house hasn't been spruced up since Mr McGee took off, and there's nothing fresh about its contents.

Three of them are now collapsed like ragdolls against each other on the couch. Una is at one end, her long legs crossed over on a mismatched pouf in front of her, her mouth agape, Tessa asleep at the other, chin in her bosom, and between them Roco, his head on Tessa's lap, his legs across Una's knees, snoring loudly.

I never minded his snoring, not like other couples. I knew he couldn't help it, just like I can't help looking down on them fondly despite their secrecy, despite their lies.

The others have left, and Mrs McGee is back in her own bed, sleeping soundly. It's sad and all, but it's clear from my friends' proximity to each other that whatever Una has told them, whatever her secrets—my dad? Thailand? Her friendship with a suspected killer?—all is now forgiven.

I am both relieved and insulted, but I let them be. I pull

myself away and return to my house where I see the police have left as promised and my folks are still awake. I know it's petulant of me, but I guess I'd feel betrayed if they were snoring happily.

Nobody wants their death to send people to sleep.

Mum and Dad are huddled under separate blankets in separate chairs in their own living room, clutching what looks like tumblers of whisky, their eyes still wide with the horror of it all, but the boys are nowhere to be seen. I assume Paul has returned to his own family, and as for Peter? God knows. Is he a black splotch again? Has he found another hotel room, another warm body to help him through?

Then I hear a loud snore followed by a moan and a splutter, and I almost giggle. I feel like a little girl again, peeping in on her big brother. Peter's under that duvet in the guest bedroom, his clothes strewn on the floor, an empty crystal tumbler on the bedside table. For the first time in ten years he has stayed over at my parents' place. It's a pity I had to die for that to happen.

I wonder about this now.

Why *did* Peter stay away so often? Why does he live his life as if from behind a shadow?

"He can shag and snort and do whatever he likes at the InterContinental," Paul had mumbled the last time he came to town, but I didn't think that was it. I had a hunch there was something deeper going on.

I wonder now if he knew about Dad and Una, if he'd caught Dad sleeping around with other women in the past. Was that what he was avoiding? Or is it something else entirely?

"Could be gay?" Neal says, catching me by surprise, but I don't bother to look around.

He seems to be popping up more frequently now, and I'm slowly getting used to it.

"He's not gay."

"How do you know?"

"He might not be married, but there's always a girl on the scene."

"Ah, the classic gay beard! A ruse! Maybe that's why he lives in London, so he can hide his true self."

Finally I turn to face him, my head cocked.

"All right then," he says, "if you say so. Pity though. He's a hunk, that one."

"What do you want, Neal?"

"Deseree asked me to come out, see if I can help speed things along."

"I thought I had all the time in the world. What happened to that?"

"You do have time. But you don't need it, honey. You just need to open your eyes and see."

"I am!" I snap back. "My eyes are so open I'm seeing shit that, quite frankly, I wish I'd never seen! I would have been very happy to head off to Forever without any of this, so you can tell Deseree to—"

Diiing, ding, diiiiiiing!

A high-pitched bell breaks through my tantrum, and I look back down. I know that ringtone. I'd tune into it at a heavy metal concert. It's my front doorbell. Ruth and Kelly are standing outside, finally acting like the intruders they are and not the owners of the place, startling my parents in the process.

They both jump, and Dad manages to spill whisky all over his blanket.

"Bugger it," he says.

Mum looks at the clock on the wall. It's just after eight. How did that happen? She sighs heavily. "I'll get it."

As she makes her way to the front of the house, her stoicism reminds me of something, of another time. She closes her eyes very briefly, then opens them again as she swings open the door, waving Ruth in without a word. She doesn't ask what she wants. She doesn't have to. She's been waiting for their return.

Kelly remains outside as Ruth and Mum walk back to the lounge room where Dad is now gathering dirty glasses and soggy paper plates and attempting to clean up. I had forgotten all about my party and am almost taken aback by the mess, which looks excessive in the harsh light of day. The empty champagne flutes and lurid-coloured cupcakes, some stabbed with cigarette butts, seem so out of place under the circumstances. Like a really lame joke.

"Can I have a word with you both?" Ruth says, and Dad drops a beer bottle back into the potted plant where he found it.

They sit down on the couch together now and wait.

Ruth glances at Mum, shoots her a look I can't read, before turning to Dad. "I've just spoken with my counterpart in customs, Mr May. We know all about your recent trip to Thailand," she tells him.

I think, *Yes, yes, that's old news, move it along!*

"We know who you were there with, and we know why you went."

Now Dad closes his eyes and hangs his head, and my heart crumbles all over again. Is this how my poor mother has to learn of his affair? Does Ruth really need to make it so brutal?

Mum is staring at Ruth, but I can't read her face. I can't read her mind.

Before the detective can say anything else, three things happen. Ruth gets a call on her phone and holds a finger up to excuse herself, my brother Paul enters the room, his car keys jangling, and Mum turns to Dad and says, "Say nothing."

Then she plasters a smile to her face, turns to Paul and says, "Cup of tea darling?"

CHAPTER 23

As the kettle begins the boiling process (gee it's been getting a workout), Mum reaches for some loose-leaf tea and begins to make a pot, calling back to Paul.

"You're up early, sweetie."

He looks like he hasn't even been to bed, and he wipes a hand across his advancing stubble.

"Well, the little ones are always up at the crack of dawn so…"

He slumps onto a stool. I wish he wouldn't do that. I wish he'd return to the living room and sit beside our shaking dad. Or at the very least start cleaning the mess up, because I know that it will be left to Mum, and I feel so guilty about that. And I'm not talking about the dirty wineglasses.

Dad has somehow pulled himself together and enters the kitchen. He gives Paul's shoulder a squeeze before dropping into the neighbouring stool.

"So Pete's still asleep, is he?" Paul mutters. "Well what a surprise. Typical."

"Don't."

It's a simple word, but it's loaded with emotion. Both Dad and Paul look up at Mum with a start. She has her back to them, but we can all tell she is at breaking point.

"Just today," she says slowly, her voice low and firm, "can we just have peace, please? That's all I ask."

141

Paul looks away, shamefaced, and I wonder about that. Did we fight all the time? Were we really that kind of family? That's not what I recall or, at least, not entirely.

I have a strong memory of giggling with my brothers, only recently in fact. I remember perching on my bed, Paul at the door, Peter by my side, the laptop in front of him as we snorted with laughter. We joked about dressing up and hitting nightclubs and getting "out of it" together.

There was a lot of love and laughter between the fighting and the angst. Wasn't there?

Ruth is now in the kitchen too, Kelly by her side. She nods hello to Paul as she slips her phone back into her pocket. She appears to have forgotten her line of questioning because she says nothing further about Thailand. Instead, she asks, "Have any of you had any interaction at all with Dr Vijay Singh?"

Paul's the only one that looks at her blankly now, but I'm more confused than ever. What's Tall, Dark and Handsome got to do with Thailand?

"You mentioned him last night," says Mum, now facing the detective. "Who is he? What's going on?"

"I just need to clarify whether you've ever met him, had any conversations or correspondence with him. I need to know the truth."

"No, we told you that yesterday," she says. "But why? Why are you asking us that?"

"Never mind," is Ruth's clipped reply, but my mum does mind, very much. She has abandoned the tea and is staring hard at the detective, arms on her hips.

"Is that man involved? Is that what you're saying?"

Ruth looks at her patiently and seems to wrestle with an answer. Eventually she says, "Dr Singh has been at the scene of two other apparent suicides in the past eighteen months. His presence here is therefore somewhat suspicious."

"Why was he here?" Mum demands. "Who brought him?"

"One of the guests."

"Which one?"

Again with the hesitation, then, "Una Conway."

Mum's eyes shoot straight to Dad, who is not looking up. Again. I wonder if he has any idea how shifty he looks? *Has* looked ever since he got home.

Paul says, "Who is this bozo? What's going on?"

Another good question, thanks, Paul! I thought we'd eliminated that bozo. Five seconds ago he had a rock-solid alibi. Did Craig get that bit wrong? Did some new information come in?

Ruth draws away from the bench. "I need to check something in your daughter's room, Mrs May."

Mum blinks back at her, surprised by the subject change. "Um... sure... fine," she stammers, before staring back at Dad.

The detective glances between them, then turns and departs the kitchen, heading up the stairs towards my bedroom, her lapdog nipping at her heels.

"What did Una do?" I hear Mum ask, her voice quivering now, like she is only just controlling her anger.

"I don't know," Dad whispers.

"You promised me you'd leave it alone!" she says, the control faltering. "You said it was a mistake, that it was over."

"It was! I had nothing to do with that." He looks up, his eyes stricken. Every wrinkle on his face seems etched in charcoal, deeper, darker, almost gothic. "You think I would allow this? While we're not here? You think I would let that man...?"

Mum's eyes narrow. "What? Let that man *what*?" Dad looks away again and Paul glances between them, worried.

"What's going on, Mum? Dad?"

Mum folds her arms across her chest. "I don't know what to think anymore, David. It's a bloody mess." And then she hisses. "You made it messy. It didn't need to be!"

Mum's hiss cuts through to Ruth, who stops on the staircase and considers returning before seeing Mum storm past and out to the pool, a hand across her mouth like she's smothering the screams or the sobs or something.

Ruth resumes her climb upwards.

My bedroom is a mess. The police have clearly ransacked it. I may not have unpacked properly, but I have always been neat and tidy. One glance at my room and you would think I was a slob. I am irate. How dare the police destroy my last resting place! (And no, I don't count Dad's study; there was no resting going on in there.)

Ruth tells Kelly to wait at the door, then steps inside. She takes a moment to look around, then strides across to my bed, lifts up the pillow, then the quilt to look underneath. I have no idea what she's looking for, but all I can see are fresh sheets and a lavender wheat pack. She bites her lower lip, then leans down and plunges one hand between the mattress and the wall. She fumbles around for a bit and then pulls out a semitransparent green plastic folder. There's something inside—is that paper? Brochures? She glances at the folder briefly, flashes Kelly a victory smile, then wedges the folder under one arm and retreats.

What the hell was that? Why are things being stashed down walls all of a sudden? I don't recall putting that there. How did she find it, or more specifically, how did she know to look there?

The plot thickens again, and I am more lost than ever.

CHAPTER 24

With a mug of tea in each hand, Paul steps out to the back deck and looks around. Mum is perched on the daybed, knees up, arms wrapped around her legs, fat tears dropping from her eyes. She sponges them up with a tissue as Paul closes in.

He hands her a cup.

"Thanks, love," she says, sniffing into her Kleenex.

"No worries."

He repositions some cushions and drops down beside her. And they sit like that for a bit, both sipping their tea, him staring out to the pool, looking constipated again. I know he's confused. I know he has no clue what just happened, yet he doesn't want to ask. I can feel his hesitation. And it annoys the hell out of me.

Ask, you idiot! Find out! Stop being the evasive ostrich you've always been!

I love Paul, can't help that fact, but he's always hidden from life, taken as few risks as possible. That's why he married the first girl he met and had kids as soon as possible and lost himself in suburbia, six blocks down from his childhood house. For all his sleazing, for all his sins, at least Peter got out, got a career, got stuck into life. Paul just treads water, and right now all that treading is getting us nowhere.

I used to admire his steady reticence once. I got it. I had a dash of it myself. Now it irritates me. I need him to butt in. I need him to interrogate our mother. She knows something. Dad knows something too. *We* need to know what that is.

"You okay, Mum?" he eventually asks, and she sniffs again, then turns and offers him a comforting smile.

I love the way she tries to comfort others when she's so clearly in turmoil.

"Really?" he persists.

Good, I think, keep going!

"'Course, yes, this isn't going to break me, honey." Then her smile firms up. "It won't break *you* either, or your Dad. We'll be okay."

Like he's the one who needs consoling. He nods but does not look like he agrees.

Then I hear his thoughts. Thoughts I wish he didn't want me to hear.

Fuck you, Maisie. Look what you've done.

I look away, I race away, I don't want to hear those thoughts. Victim blaming is one thing but from my own brother, my own flesh and blood! I'm sorry my murder has left a gaping hole and you're all confused and hurting, but really, Paul? Really?

It's like I've been shot all over again.

I shift away from the pool. I wander my old street, or at least as far as I can go. I see one set of neighbours heading off somewhere, hats on their heads. They're smiling like it's a new day, and I guess, for them—for everyone but me—it is. I see old Mrs Russo has swapped her floral nightie for a floral muumuu and is reaching for the rolled newspaper on her lawn. I'm sure my murder hasn't made that early edition, but she's ripping the plastic off, scanning the front pages. Is she looking for coverage of my death or just checking the weather report?

I see a blue heeler galloping towards her. That dog looks familiar. I stop and watch for a bit.

"Kasper! Kasp! Here boy! Come!"

There's a middle-aged man standing at the end of the road, a dark beanie on his head, muddy leash in his hands, and Mrs Russo steps back, wary, as the dog rushes up. But it just gives her a cursory sniff before turning back.

"Good boy!" the man yells and holds a palm out to the woman. "Sorry about that!"

She gives him a curt nod, then shuffles back up her path.

I look at the man. He, too, looks familiar. I know I've seen him before. Why's he wearing a woollen beanie? It's already hot out.

"Oi! You!"

Roco is striding across the McGee's front lawn, his clothes cruddy, his hair tufted up like a crazed clown, congealed blood just visible between his shirt and neck. He looks like the walking dead, and the man glances at him with a start, then grabs his dog's collar and pulls him close.

Roco notices the dog and slows his pace.

"Can I help you?" the man says, dropping down to pat his stocky mutt's white-and-bluish-black coat.

"You came to the party last night; you were making threats," Roco says, and the man gets back up, one hand still wrapped around his dog's collar.

"The music was loud," he replies. "I just wanted the music down."

"You were going to call the cops."

"But I didn't." Then he frowns. "Perhaps I should have."

Roco stops, scowls, places his hands on his hips. "What does that mean?"

"I heard what happened to that poor girl. The police came to my door."

Roco's scowl deepens. He glances around the street, then back at the man and says, "Did you do it? Did you kill my friend?"

And there it is. He's officially disowned me three times. *Not that I'm counting.*

The man reels back now, his dog barking at the sudden movement. "What? Are you insane? Why would you say that?"

"Because you were angry, mate. You were making threats!"

"I told you, it was late, I wanted the music off, and I didn't think it was good for..." He lets that sentence dangle and pulls his beanie off. "Look, that's all it was, okay? Why would I shoot somebody? Over *music*?"

Roco stares hard at him now, but his tone is slightly calmer as he repeats the words, "But you were angry." Then, shockingly he says, "I saw you, man. I saw you talking to Maisie."

The man stiffens considerably then, and sensing this, his dog begins to growl. "I just asked her to turn the music down. She said she would, and then I left."

"How do I know that?" Roco says, his tone darkening again. "It's the last time I saw her alive. How do I know you didn't do it?"

I notice old Mrs Russo has not gone back inside; she is loitering by her door, listening in.

The man notices, too, and has had enough. He leans down and attaches the leash to the dog's collar. "I didn't kill anybody." He looks back at Roco and shakes his head. "Get a grip, lad. Maybe you and your mates need to ask yourselves what *you* were doing when it happened. Take a good, hard look at yourselves."

Then he pulls the leash tight and says, "Come on, Kasper."

Roco watches them depart, his arms now dangling by his side, as if he's been deflated. He's not sure whether to believe him, but I do. The memory is now as clear as the sunlight filtering through the flame tree overhead, and the man with the Blue Heeler is right.

He *did* come to the house last night. I remember it now. It's suddenly very, very clear. That man appeared just as my mother's phone text came through.

Neighbours worried, hun. Have u got people over? Everything okay?

Except the 'okay' was a 'thumbs-up' emoji, and I remember being surprised. Mum was adapting faster than I thought.

Before I could respond to her message, I heard a strange sound, a dog bark, and I looked up from the pool and back into the house. There was a man standing just inside the front door, his lanky frame silhouetted by the entrance light. He had his dog by his side and a phone in his hand. I'd seen him before, walking his dog in the street.

"I've just spoken to your folks," he told me when I made my way in. "They're not happy about the party, and neither am I. It's not good."

"I'm sorry," I told him. I begged him not to call the police.

"I'll let it go for now," he said. "Out of respect for Mandy and David and, well, everything that's going on." He couldn't meet my eyes then as he shifted on his feet. "But it's very late and you need to turn that music down and get some rest."

I promised I would and bid him good night.

I bid him good night. I am sure of it. I am sure—aren't I?—that he left the premises. Then I started down the hallway, determined not just to turn down the music but to turf everybody out. I was tired. Enough was enough. I'd tried to stop the party earlier, but my friends had laughed me off. Now I'd show them all I was serious, yet something stopped me. Something happened.

Yes, I remember! *Something caught my eye!*

Instead of heading back to the pool, I took a detour, to the right of the front door, in the direction of the study.

What was it? What made me take that fatal detour, the last detour of my life?

CHAPTER 25

A high-pitched screech shakes the memory away, and I see yet another kettle rattle at boiling point. It's in the McGee kitchen this time, and Tammie is padding quickly towards it, looking panicked. She wants to shut it off before she "wakes the dead"—her thoughts, not mine.

Why do women of a certain age assume a hot cup of tea will solve everything, heal all wounds, I wonder? And are they right? Is it as simple as that?

As she pours the water into a chipped teapot, Una appears looking less dishevelled than Roco but equally as shell-shocked.

"Coffee," she mutters, her voice like a hung-over smoker. "I need coffee."

Tammie nods towards a high shelf where a plunger sits, then crosses to the pantry and pulls out a tin. Una retrieves the plunger, takes the tin, opens it and shakes some ground coffee in.

As she waits for Tammie to refill the kettle and start the boiling process again, she glances out the kitchen window towards my house and flinches. She looks at Mrs McGee, who is now pulling out a frying pan, a carton of eggs on the bench top.

Una wraps her wrinkled jacket tighter around her waist then deserts the kettle and opens the side kitchen door, rushing out. I assume she is heading for Roco, who is now seated on a mouldy lawn chair, head in his hands.

Is he weeping?

We don't get a chance to find out. Una completely bypasses him and is striding down the McGee driveway and across the road in the direction of my house, her eyes staring straight ahead. She looks determined, but she also looks nervous. She scrapes fingers through her long tresses as she goes, wipes the sleep from her eyes.

I see what Una is looking at now. Who. It's my dad, and he is standing at the bottom of the driveway, dropping glass bottles into the recycling bin. He sees her, stops and waits for her to cross over, his face a blank mask.

Are they really going to do this now? With my mother sobbing by the pool and detectives crawling the place?

"David," Una says stiffly. She offers him a grim smile when she gets closer. "I'm so, so sorry."

He does not smile back.

"Why did you bring him?" Dad bursts out, and she looks surprised by this. It is not what she is expecting, yet she knows who he means because she answers quickly.

"I didn't realise. I didn't think."

"You could get us into big trouble, Una. It's not over, you know? This whole thing could blow up."

"It won't. We didn't do anything. We're innocent. They've got nothing on us."

"Bullshit," he spits, and I recoil.

I have never heard my father use language like that, certainly not to a woman. He coughs, clears his throat. Settles his temper down.

"Sorry, Una." He takes a deep breath. "Sorry, but it was stupid. The whole thing was stupid. I don't know how you talked me into it. I don't know how I could possibly have gone through with it."

"You were coming from a place of love," she says. "We both were—"

"I wasn't thinking! I was a fool."

"I know, I'm sorry…" She goes to reach out to him, but he has backed away.

He shakes his head, his whole body shaking alongside it, then he smashes the last bottle into the bin and strides back up the driveway.

"Wait!" she calls out, and he stops, his back to her. "I left you something. On your desk. Did you get it?"

She can't see his face, but I can. He looks puzzled but I'm not.

She left you a love letter, you idiot! She penned you sweet nothings and left it on your desk for Mum to find. Probably reminiscing about your romantic rendezvous in Thailand. The cow.

But hang on. That doesn't add up.

Una has that love letter in her pocket, doesn't she? Vijay swiped it from Dad's desk last night and handed it back to her a few hours ago. I saw him!

So what's Una talking about? Is it that boarding pass? Was she returning it?

"I need to talk to you," she persists. "I need to show you something—"

"Later!" he growls, still not looking at her.

"But it's important, David, you'll want to—"

"I said later!"

"But, David—"

"Una, *please!*" He's facing her now, and his fury has morphed into despair. He looks across to her like a small child premeltdown, his lower lip quivering, his eyes swelling up. "Please, Una. Whatever it is, I can't face it now. I just can't…"

Then he turns and shuffles like a geriatric up the driveway.

Detective Ruth is standing at the top, just by the front door. She has seen the whole thing, although what she has heard I cannot tell. Dad stops when he sees her, then growls something unintelligible to himself and continues walking, scooping up the day's newspaper before sweeping past her and into the house.

In the kitchen he tosses the rolled-up paper on the bench and throws open the fridge. As he stares into it, not hungry, not really seeing the contents, Ruth approaches.

"You want to tell me about Thailand now, Mr May? About your trip with Ms Conway?" Her tone is mild but firm.

Mum is still at the pool with Paul. Seems as good a time as ever.

He slams the door shut, turns and then leans against it.

"It was a mistake."

"Actually, it was a lot more than that. It's a federal offence."

Adultery? Since when?

He flinches. "We didn't go ahead with it. You must know that."

"I know nothing of the sort. I'm supposed to just believe you, am I?"

He blinks back tears, his throat now choked. "Believe what the hell you want. I loved her. I loved her deeply." His voice cracks.

"Enough to commit murder, Mr May?"

His eyes flood with something I can't quite recognise. Is it guilt? Regret?

Then he surprises me by smiling, but it's not a happy smile. It is giddy and ugly and full of shame. "That's the sad irony, Detective Powell. Despite everything, I clearly didn't love her enough."

Then he slides down the fridge to the floor, drops his head into his chest and weeps like a baby.

My heart is shattering, shattering, shattering, but I have no time to pick up the pieces or put any of that together because another squad car has just pulled up out the front. I watch with misery as Craig and the ponytailed officer step out. What was her name again? Did we ever find out? The woman remains by the car while Craig walks up the driveway and lets himself straight in the house.

It's amazing how quickly the force take over your home when a crime has occurred. How politeness and protocol are so quickly abandoned.

He finds Ruth in the kitchen, squatting down, patting Dad's back. Their eyes lock, and she gets up. She steps out of the kitchen and down the hallway.

"He all right?" Craig asks, which is touching, I suppose, but she waves him on. As I said, there's no time for that shit.

He pulls something from his jacket, several A4 pages stapled together.

"Just got the pathologist's preliminary report," he says, thrusting it towards her. "Brought it straight over."

She snatches the sheets from him and scans the details. Frowns.

"That's not the best bit," he says. "Read the next page."

She turns to the next sheet and continues reading, her eyebrows lifting, her head nodding suddenly.

"It was on her breasts," he says, sounding excited. "Only one set of fingerprints, and it's a match. Should we have pulled her top down last night and found it ourselves?"

"No, no," Ruth replies, sounding eerily calm while my mind starts spinning in all sorts of directions, most of them pretty horrendous.

What are they talking about? Why would they need to pull my top down? What did they find on my breasts of all places? Did the killer scribble something? Leave a calling card?

Ruth doesn't look at all perturbed, if anything she looks rather pleased by all this. Then she has the audacity to say, "Okay. Good. She took her own life. Well that's a relief."

Say, what?

I give my head a metaphorical shake. I try to let those words sink in.

She. Took. Her. Own. Life.

Er, no, Detective. No I bloody didn't!

"Let's pack up," Ruth is saying. "Let's get this finalised."

I turn and glare at the tunnel, which is infuriatingly empty again. Where is smug boy now? Where is the condescending middle-aged chick?

How many times do I have to tell you people! I did not kill myself! I would not do that to my family, to my loved ones!

And, frankly, I am outraged that the lead investigator now believes I did.

I try to scramble my thoughts together. Why isn't Ruth thinking clearly? There is so much evidence, so many suspects, and I'm not just talking this latest snippet, which has got me in a fluster. *What on earth could they possibly have found on my breasts? And whose fingerprints are they talking about?*

Forget that for now. We have plenty more to work with.

What about the dodgy "doctor" who has a history of murder and been up on multiple charges? I thought Una must have inadvertently brought him over, but maybe there was nothing inadvertent about it. We've all been preoccupied with pathetic pink envelopes and extramarital antics, but now the memory of all those hundred dollar bills flashes back. I know Vijay swiped that envelope. Did he also take the cash? Or did it belong to him? Did he earn it somehow? Did he then ditch it down the sofa to avoid incrimination?

I know it sounds outlandish, but what if Vijay was a hired gun? What if Una hired him for some reason? I'm not saying she hired him to kill me, but maybe I got in the way?

All right, it's beyond crazy, it's ludicrous. Let's forget about him for a moment and put the whole ugly Vijay-Una-Dad combo to one side. We still have half a dozen suspects who haven't been properly scrutinised.

What about that aggressive neighbour with the blue dog? Did anyone stop to investigate his background? He came into my house. He threatened me. Did he follow me into Dad's office and leave his mark, in more ways than one?

What about my brothers? Come on, how suspicious have they been acting? I know they love me—I get that—but it doesn't mean they didn't do this thing. They clearly had their own troubles; they clearly begrudged the help my parents were giving me. I wonder now if Dad was selling Nevercloud, not for Mum but to help *me*. Is that why they are so angry with me? Is that why it's all Peter can think about now?

Has anyone looked into their recent financial records? Paul's family is growing bigger by the day, yet he just downshifted to a shoebox. Has he lost his job? Is he broke? That's got to eat away at you while you watch your baby sister laze about in the family palace.

Not to mention Mr so-called Moneybags. Why was Peter staying in a two-bit hotel and using public transport when five-star and business-class are more his style? Does he, too, have money issues, or does he have a drug problem he needs to finance? I can still hear Paul's words, like a slap across Peter's face.

"What were you doing last night? Pulling chicks? Scoring a hit?"

Was Peter's drug problem back?

I have a strong memory of giggling… Peter by my side, the laptop in front of him as we snorted with laughter. We joked about dressing up and hitting nightclubs and getting "out of it" together.

Was that why he was at a dingy train station in the dead of night? Was he getting out of it to get over the trauma of what he'd done?

And what about Arabella? Maybe she's no innocent! Maybe she *was* in it with Dr Vijay, giving him the fake alibi he required. Maybe she's just pretending to be a jilted lover to cover her tracks.

What about Tessa and Roco and their obvious love affair?

Or Leslie or Jonas for that matter…

There were almost a hundred people at my house last

night. Surely one of them could have done this thing. Surely we can't rest the case this quickly!

There is no way, dear reader, that I took that gun to my own head and fired that shot for no good reason. And, frankly, I'm offended that anyone would even consider it. I have no choice now. I have to try harder to remember.

Think, Maisie, think!

Go back to ground zero.

Go back to the moment you died.

There was someone in my Dad's office last night, I just know it. I didn't go in there to kill myself. I went in to see who had turned on the light.

And I did see! I must have! Just like I know somebody else rolled that office chair across to the wall, closer to that gun. *It wasn't me. I know it wasn't.*

Yet the memory remains just out of reach, and the answer feels like it's a million miles away.

CHAPTER 26

DS Powell is issuing orders. Kelly is to gather my entire family in the living room. But it will be a party of a different kind.

As he does that—asking Mum to wake Peter, even getting Paul to call his wife—I sneak another glance towards the McGee household. Roco has returned inside and is hooking into greasy bacon and eggs with little more than hunger on his mind while Mrs McGee watches him wistfully, thinking how lovely it would be to have a man in the house again.

Tessa has woken and is slumped at a kitchen stool, wishing she'd stuck with the mocktails Arabella was whipping up instead of spiking them with tequila. Una is on the stool opposite her, staring at the fridge, the coffee plunger now empty in her hands. She is thinking, *I need another coffee. I haven't got the strength yet.*

They're no use to me. Their thoughts have all moved on, and so I go back home. I go back to my mother.

Sometime in the past ten minutes—or was it thirty?—she has showered and changed into fresh clothes. She looks better, almost normal, and this time I'm glad of it. She's going to need her wits about her. Ruth's news will hit her like a rock in the head. Seated beside Mum on the living room couch, Dad still looks a mess. He can't find the energy to do anything but chew at his bottom lip. Like father like son, I guess.

Peter has appeared and is clutching a can of Coke like his life depends upon it, and Paul is sitting across from him, his brow wrinkled again, his wife at his feet. I don't know where their kids are, but I'm glad they're not here. This is no business for young children.

My mind flits suddenly to another child, a cheeky smile, a smothered giggle, but it is lost again as Ruth claps loudly.

"Okay, people, thanks for coming."

Like she's Lady Muck and they are the visiting peasants.

Ruth is standing in the centre of my living room, her shoulders straight, her hands behind her back. Now she looks like Hercule Poirot about to deliver the climactic denouement, all eyes are upon her, including my own.

I think I know what she is going to say, so I am thrown completely when she produces a plastic folder and waves it about.

"I don't know who colluded here, who knew what," she begins, "and frankly, I'm not sure I want to know. This is tragic enough."

Sorry, what?

She slaps the green plastic folder on the coffee table dismissively and turns to Kelly, one hand out. He has two sets of printouts and hands one across.

"First," she says, "we have checked the fingerprints on the pistol. Apart from Mr May's, which we'd expect to find"—she shoots my worried father a glance—"there were no other prints but Maisie's."

Then, in case they didn't get it, she looks at each of them in turn as she says, "Maisie is the only other person who touched that gun. We also found gun residue on her right hand."

They all nod, like that's perfectly acceptable, but I can't believe what I'm hearing. I've read enough murder mysteries. The killer could easily have wiped away his prints before smudging mine on postmortem. As for the residue? Perhaps I raised my hand as the gun went off.

She looks at Kelly, and he passes across the second printout. "Even better for you lot, we have some preliminary tox results, and they've come back clean. Maisie did not have anything in her system, no drugs, no alcohol, nothing."

Again they all nod, but this time their relief is palpable while my head is left spinning. That bit most certainly does not add up. I remember being shaky on my feet, slopping margaritas about the place. They must have found *something* in my system. How do they explain that?

Mum is nodding like a yo-yo, and Dad has his hands at his mouth as if trying not to say what he is thinking, which is *Thank God*.

Ruth is not quite finished yet. "That does not explain, however, why we found these in the pool toilet."

She produces the evidence bag with the illegal drugs and drops it onto the table, on top of that plastic folder.

Dad's relief vanishes as quickly as it came. Mum turns to look at him, and he recoils under her gaze.

"I didn't buy those, honey, I promise—"

A throat clears. "It's okay, Dad," says Peter. "It was me."

"Shut up, Peter!" growls Paul as his wife nestles into his legs as though hoping to block the whole ugly saga out.

"No, you shut up, mate. I've had enough of all the lies." He looks directly at Ruth. "I helped her find them online. She asked me. I had to help."

Mum looks at him aghast, but that box looks suddenly familiar and now more of my memory is clicking into place. *That's* what we were doing with the computer on my bed. We were ordering those drugs online. No, actually, *he* was. It was his credit card, his laptop.

Ruth says, "The seal has not been broken. They are unopened."

She is addressing this to my mother, who looks marginally relieved. "That does not detract from the fact that it is an offence to solicit pentobarbitals over the internet."

Pento-what?

"I'd do it again," Peter says defiantly. "In a fucking heartbeat."

"Peter!" Mum cries out, but I'm not sure if she's upset by the swear word or the sentiment.

"She was *depressed* Mum, she was *miserable*, it was the kindest thing."

Dad nods at him, over and over. Now he's turned into the yo-yo. "Good on ya, Peto," he growls. "Good on ya, mate."

What's going on? Why is my family so keen to drug me? To see me get out of my mind? Was I really that miserable? Was I really that depressed?

"But I let her down, Mum," Peter is saying, his eyes welling up. "I was supposed to leave them by her bedside. But I didn't. We…" He looks at Paul, whose eyes are firmly shut, Jan's the size of saucers below him. "We were going to hold her hand through it, yeah? But… but Paul's kids got sick and he couldn't make it and we agreed to put it off."

Paul shifts in his seat. His eyes remain shut. "My kids weren't that sick," he mumbles. "I just… I just couldn't."

Peter sniffs like he already knew that and then stares at his lap.

Ruth does not seem at all surprised by this outburst, but she's not particularly pleased by it either. She waits a few moments, then she says, "Which brings us back to last night. I have a theory if you'd like to hear it."

All eyes are back upon her.

"As I said before, I don't know who was colluding with whom, and who was planning what, but I think your daughter saw an opportunity and she took it."

"The gun," Dad says.

"The gun," she repeats. "These pills may have been her first option, but something changed her mind. I believe Maisie saw the gun, made a snap decision and took her own life."

They are all yo-yos now, their relief intensifying with each nod, and I want to scream and rail and thump my fists at their stupid bouncing heads.

I want to shout *"But I wouldn't do this to myself! I wouldn't!"*

Dad asks, "And Una's friend? That man, Vijay?"

"We don't believe he was involved, Mr May. Not this time. We've checked and double-checked the witness statements. He was never alone with your daughter, and we don't believe he was involved in this particular suicide, at least not directly."

Again, they nod as though this is a perfectly reasonable assumption.

Ruth reaches down and retrieves the pill packet and the green folder. It's the one she found down the side of my bed, but she never even explained what was in it, and nobody seems even remotely interested in asking. As she hands it across to Kelly, I try desperately to read the sheets inside, but again it all looks like hieroglyphics to me.

Why? Why? Why!

"What happens now?" someone asks. Paul's wife, I think.

Ruth glances back at her as she exits the living room.

"Now you organise the funeral," she says gently. "Now you grieve."

CHAPTER 27

I stand alone in the middle of nothing. Bleak. Bereft. Befuddled.

Am I really to believe I killed myself? Is that all there was to it?

Maybe the truth was never going to make sense. Maybe that's why I couldn't remember. Maybe that's why I refused to accept.

I smooth down my blue jumpsuit, straighten my tiara and glance towards the tunnel. *Hello? Where are the dancing girls? Where is the marching band?*

I know what happened now, so why aren't they dragging me across?

"Because you need to see it all, the good bits and the bad."

That's Deseree, and I am so glad of her presence. I'd hug her if I had any strength left.

"What do you mean?" I say. "What bad bits? I had a secure home, loved ones, friends who cared. I could have been born in an impoverished African village. Instead, I fell apart at the first hurdle! I thought I was a little more resilient than that. I used to be the one in control. I was the one that kept the family together!"

"And that's why you had to do it, don't you see, Maisie?"

"No, that's the thing! I don't see! I still can't remember! How can I not remember taking a gun and putting a bullet into my head?"

Deseree gives me a sad, sad smile. "Because you are still not ready to accept what you have done and who you really are. It's like you forgot that bit the moment the bullet left the gun. Go back and look at yourself more closely."

"I know who I am! I'm the ditz who blows her brains out because she can't keep a boyfriend or a job."

"No, before Roco, before the job. Who were you from your earliest days?"

"Oh you mean the little brat who forced her poor brothers to play stupid games and told lame jokes and bossed everybody about. I was an annoying little snot."

"Snot of a different kind." She smiles at herself. "You were the glue, Maisie. You were the one who held them all together."

"So why kill myself?"

"Because you're still holding them together, don't you see that? You did it for them."

"What rubbish! Suicide is selfish; it's never a good thing. Look at them down there. They're distraught. I've torn them apart."

"No, honey. You had nothing but love in your heart."

"That doesn't make any sense! Was I really so miserable I was destroying the rest of them at the same time? I don't understand what you mean by that."

"Then you're not ready, my darling. You need to go back. Just for a little longer. You need to go back and really see. You need to face the truth."

I need to snot you in the face, I think as I draw myself away and drag myself back. Why can't they just let me rest? The tunnel light still shimmers; it's not so garish anymore. It flickers and teases. It lures me in.

Have I not been through enough? Can't I just cross?

Down at the pool yet another party has begun, and it seems I am forced to join in, even though the last thing I feel like is company—at least not the living, breathing kind.

Paul's kids have arrived, all four wearing matching beanies—what is it with everybody today? It's midsummer for goodness' sake. Jan's mother must have brought them all over. She's now sitting on the daybed. I wish I could remember her name. How shameful. Paul and Jan have been together fifteen years, and I can't even remember the mother-in-law's name.

Deseree is full of crap. I was a dreadful sister. A dreadful person.

Jan is sitting beside her mum, the youngest child, the sick baby, lying between them, fast asleep. I watch as the two middle kids run around the back garden, one of them stopping to rattle the pool gate, the other naked, apart from the beanie, and reaching for the pink flamingo which has been wedged between the fronds of a palm.

Dad's barbecue is starting to hiss and spurt, my brothers standing to attention beside it, Paul with metal tongs, Peter still clutching a Coke, while Dad appears from inside, a tray of sausages in his hands, Mum just behind him with some onions and a loaf of bread.

Is that it? *Really?* A few firm words from a detective and everyone gets on with their lives?

I watch as one of Paul's boys, four-year-old Toby, gives up on the gate and dashes off, giggling like he's drunk, and I'm about to look away, their fun too painful, their laughter like razor blades through my heart, when a creepy scraping sound pulls me back.

Toby has stopped giggling and is now pulling one of the deck chairs across the pavers and towards the pool gate. I'm not sure he should be doing that. I'm pretty sure he can't swim. I glance back to his mother and then to his dad, but they are both moving swiftly towards Mum.

They are going in the wrong direction.

Now they are huddled in a circle around Mum, and Peter is there and Tessa and Roco. When did they get here? And who is that in the middle of the throng?

I cannot believe my eyes. It's Una and she has the pink envelope in her hand.

How is Una welcome in this house? And why is Mum smiling at her and sobbing instead of ripping her eyes out?

I hear another giggle. I glance back towards the pool. Toby has scrambled up on the chair and is now reaching for the latch on the gate. He almost has it open.

Wake up, Paul! Turn around Jan! Somebody? Anybody! Get your eyes off that dreaded pink envelope!

Help!

I see Jan's mother glance up from the baby and towards the pool.

I hear someone cry out, "No! Get down!"

But the person crying out is me, and I am standing at the doorway to my father's study, staring at the interior wall.

I see a little boy's feet. He is standing on his tippy-toes, his swimming trunks dripping water all over Dad's good leather armchair.

I go to say something, I go to chastise, then I see what he is doing, what he is reaching towards on a handmade wooden frame.

"The gun," I tell Neal who is beside me again. Of course he is. He has been beside me all along.

He nods, knowingly. "The gun," he repeats.

I close my eyes and I exhale.

Did a small child shoot me? Is that it? Was it the boy I caught sneaking over the pool fence earlier in the night? Did he wander into my dad's office and get excited by the gun? Did he pull the chair over, reach up towards it and rip it from the wall? Did I startle him, or did he do it deliberately, thinking it was a toy, pointing it at me with delight?

No, that can't be right.

Ruth said there was gun residue on my fingers,

my fingerprints on the weapon. I must have wrestled the gun from him. The gun must have gone off accidentally.

I feel an enormous weight lift. I feel lighter suddenly.

"This makes more sense now," I tell Neal. "I didn't kill myself. It was an accident!"

Then I think of the child and I am horrified for him. Will he remember any of it? Is that why he looked so traumatised as he left my house?

Although, why didn't they find the kid's fingerprints on the gun?

I shake the question away. I just don't care.

"I'm glad Ruth never connected the dots," I tell Neal now. "I want to take the fall for that poor kid. I don't know how he could possibly get over such a thing."

I expect Neal to high-five me, but he's barely even smiling. I look back, and the tunnel seems further away than ever. And it's depressingly dark again.

"You really think that's what happened?" Neal says. "That it was all just an accident?"

I frown. "Wasn't it?"

He sighs, his tone gratingly sympathetic. "So why are you still hovering here, Maisie? Why can you still not remember?"

CHAPTER 28

Day turns into night again, but I barely notice the shifting light. I have closed my eyes. I am trying my best, damn you all. I am trying very hard to remember!

What cruel world is this, to make the victim of a violent accident remember their death before they're allowed eternal peace? Why can't we forget something so traumatic? Isn't that our prerogative? Isn't that for the best?

Open your eyes, Maisie, comes a gentle voice on the wind. *Open your eyes and see.*

It's my voice, from years ago, from a calmer, simpler time.

So I force my eyelids open and I stare to the house below, and I think, *Thanks a lot Forever, thanks for torturing me.*

So it seems the young lad didn't kill me, or at least that's what Neal is saying. How then did I die? And am I really to keep watching my loved ones as they get on with the business of living?

The pool party is over, and my friends have finally scattered. Roco has vanished completely, so too Una, but I can see Tessa back in her own kitchen, preparing an Indian curry while her mother watches her fondly. I loved Tessa's curries. I forgot about that. I will never eat another of her curries again, and it makes me want to weep. I don't care whether she hooks up with Roco or ever did. I just want to hang out with my old buddy again and eat her famous butter chicken swamped in creamy Greek yogurt.

Is that it, Death? Is that what you want me to see?

I hear a scrubbing sound, and I spot Jan in my dad's study. She is crouched on the carpet, a brush in one hand, the other wiping away the tears that are gushing down her face. There's a steaming bucket of water by her side. I must confess, this surprises me. A woman I never had any time for is now taking the time to scrub my blood away, but she isn't really doing it for me. She's doing it for Mum, and she's doing it for Dad, but mostly, she's doing it for Paul so he doesn't have to face this gruesome task. Yet again, she is rescuing him.

Is that what you wanted me to see?

I think of young Toby now, and I have a sudden flash of panic, but then I find him sleeping soundly in his dad's childhood bed upstairs, his little brother coiled close beside him, his tiny fingers clinging to a ratty old teddy. I will never get to cuddle those boys again, but I'm not sure I ever cuddled them much anyway. Did my loathing for Jan trickle down to her kids?

Is that what you wanted me to see?

A one-way conversation catches my attention now, and I notice that Peter is on the phone to someone; he's shouting but he's not angry. I think it's long distance. He's discussing dates and deadlines and asking for more time. It must be his boss. I wonder if he'll get the sack thanks to me.

And just behind him, in an armchair, Paul is dozing. He looks completely at peace.

Is that what you wanted me to see?

Dad has fallen asleep, too, on the living room sofa, his snores vibrating through the house while Mum has gone upstairs and now sits on my bed, an empty green garbage bag beside her. How can Dad sleep? How can Mum find the energy to start packing me away so quickly?

Is that what you wanted me to see?

"Mum? Can I have a word?"

That's Peter, hands thrust into his pockets, his eyes swollen red.

She offers him a gentle smile and taps the mattress beside her. He shifts a few cushions as he sits down.

"It's all my fault," he says. "I let her down."

"Honey, please, we talked about this."

"No, Mum, I need to get this off my chest." He inhales deeply. Exhales. "We had a plan, Maisie, Paul and me. We were supposed to leave the stuff by her bedside, with a glass of her favourite bubbly. But I didn't." His voice cracks. "Mum, I didn't."

"I know, honey, and I'm proud of you for that. I'm not sure how I would have coped if you had been involved." Mum's voice cracks too, but he is shaking his head and swiping at his tears.

"No, you don't get it. I was a freakin' coward! It's why she went for the gun! We were going to be there for her, we were going to hold her hand through it, yeah? So she didn't go *alone*..."

He cracks on that final word and buckles over and starts to cry. I don't think I've ever seen my big brother cry, and Mum looks equally surprised. She goes to hug him, but he pushes her away and gathers himself again.

"Paul..." He clears his throat. "Paul's kids got sick, and he chickened out and he said no, let's put it off, let's not do it. But Maisie wouldn't hear of it. She said, 'Please Peto, it's time, *please*.'" He sniffs and I sniff alongside him. "Then she let me off the hook. Poor Maisie! All I had to do was put the pills by her bedside and go. She said I didn't have to stay if I couldn't handle it. It was as easy as that. I didn't even need to hold her hand. That's all she asked of me, all she wanted... and I couldn't do it! I was a fucking coward!"

He buckles over again, his cries so wrenching Dad's eyes flicker open down in the living room. Mum rubs Peter's back and waits. I can't believe she's not aghast at this outburst. I can't believe she's so calm.

Eventually Peter collects himself and says, "I didn't want her to find them. I didn't want her to do it, so I hid the pills in the downstairs toilet and I took off. I left her all alone at her party. I needed to get away. I went straight to Central. I thought…" He gulps. "I wanted to get back to Dubbo, where everything seems so simple. So black and white, you know? I wanted to get the first train out of there, but of course there wasn't one until morning, so I just *sat* there. I just sat on my hands while she…"

Again Mum goes to hug him, again he pulls away, looking more stoned than he ever has, but it's from tears and guilt and grief. "I wasn't *there* for her, Mum. *That's* why she had to reach for the gun. I'm so ashamed. I let her down. I let my beautiful baby sister down."

Finally he falls into her arms, and their cries turn into one. I am crying with them, but I am more confused than ever.

So that explains the black shadow I suppose. It explains why he couldn't face me, even in death. He somehow feels responsible, like he forced my hand. But it doesn't explain the rest. Why would my brothers collude to help me kill myself?

Even if I was that depressed, that gutless, addicted to antidepressants—whatever—why would my brothers agree to that? Why isn't Mum chastising him? Why isn't she furious that he didn't get me help, get me some decent counselling?

After many minutes, sobbing and hugging and sobbing again, Peter swipes a tissue from my bedside table and gets up. Before he goes, Mum grabs his hand and says one final thing.

"I told you before and I'll tell you until I'm blue in the face: your sister made her own choices, she did what she did willingly. And we *have* to live with that, Peter. *You* have to live with that because I have lost enough already."

I know what she is saying and so does he. He nods, tears streaming down his cheeks again. Then he nods more assuredly and walks out while Mum is left sitting on my bed, alone and bereft.

She sighs like she's ninety-five, wipes her face and looks around. Then she picks up the plastic bag and turns to my bedside table, reaching for a small white container. She scoops it up, and I hear it rattle as she drops it into the bag, then reaches for another.

There are six different bottles of pills on the table. How much medication *was* I taking? Are they all antidepressants? I look a little closer.

There's aspirin there and heavy-duty ibuprofen and something called Riluzole.

Hang on, those aren't antidepressants, and that's not our family doctor's name printed on the label. It's someone else. Dr Harry Chang, from St Vincent's Hospital.

Okay, I remember him!

I remember this!

Suddenly I recall it clearly. It was two winters ago, soon after that date with Jonas. Soon after I'd broken my leg. I was now getting twitches and cramps in my other leg, and for some reason my hands weren't working properly. I'd had enough. I needed answers.

You came with me, Mum, and for some reason so did Dad even though he hated doctors and I'd never seen him inside a hospital before.

And we sat there and we smiled, but Dr Chang wasn't smiling.

"It's not good," he said simply.

And then suddenly I see.

The horror on my parents' faces.

The reason Jonas turned and fled.

The charity fundraiser where I first met Roco; the reason I broke up with him last week.

The cups crashing on the kitchen floor, the

preoccupied mind and the lost files, the sympathetic smiles and that final handshake.

It's why I moved back home but never quite moved in. The reason my mother cooked mushy food and my father looked so damn hopeless. And why Una threw that stupid party where I stumbled about even though I wasn't drunk.

I wasn't a loser.

I wasn't depressed.

I had a disease, a dirty disease, and that's the reason I'm dead.

CHAPTER 29

"**I** don't know how to tell you this," Dr Chang said. "But at least it will help explain why you fell over, Maisie, and broke your leg."

And I thought, *It's some kind of cancer. Bone cancer probably. But I'll fight it.*

"It's motor neurone disease. MND. I'm so sorry."

I frowned. I shrugged. I'd never heard of it, but who cared? *I'll still fight it*, I thought to myself, but the terror that was creeping into my parents' eyes suggested otherwise.

Dr Google confirmed the rest. Google also called it Lou Gehrig's disease or amyotrophic lateral sclerosis (ALS), but no amount of titles could change the fact that there was no fighting this one. There was no cure, and it was beyond my control. Not even the world's bossiest sister or the most efficient PA could juggle this problem away.

I had a neurodegenerative disease that causes rapidly progressive muscle weakness. In a nutshell: my life was over before it had really taken off. I would be lucky to survive two years, five if I was unlucky. By then I'd be wheelchair-bound and unable to swallow, let alone speak. I would be completely dependent on other people, well, my parents to be precise. And I hadn't been dependent on them since I was five.

It was around that age I learned to count and decided

that while I might have been a mistake—what idiots have a third baby six years after the last?—I would not be a burden. Never that.

I was fiercely independent from then on, super bossy and determined to run my own race. And now they were telling me I'd soon lose the ability to talk and walk?

Not on my watch.

I guess I'd felt symptoms and ignored them for some time. All that smashed crockery should have been a giveaway, but the real red flag came with that clumsy fall down those restaurant stairs, Jonas watching on helpless and cringing with embarrassment. He didn't think I was *that* drunk.

For some reason Dad always blamed Jonas for my disease, like he was the catalyst. And Dad certainly blamed him for doing a runner as soon as the word got out. I didn't. I understood why Jonas didn't stick around. He barely knew me, and what he thought he knew had just been shattered, in more ways than one. Why would he want to hang around to nurse me through it? Why would I *want* him to?

I think I accepted it fairly quickly after that first diagnosis and learned how to manage the pain and my failing muscles, investing in supportive cushions and heated wheat packs and weekly sessions with an acupuncturist called Arabella, who fast became my friend.

The problem was no one else accepted it, my father least of all. He shunned the prognosis, could not believe that the disease was incurable, and began scrounging around for experimental treatments and miracle cures, each one pricier and more outlandish than the next.

Then Una told him about a "medical miracle" she'd heard about in Thailand and somehow convinced him to travel with her to investigate. When they realised it was a crock—just another snake oil salesman selling little more than water and wishes from a dirty street stall in Bangkok—they turned to Plan B and purchased some

Nembutal, aka the "peaceful pill." That's a well-known euthanasia drug, a pentobarbital, illegal Down Under yet available without prescription in Thailand. They were going to sneak it back into the country and hide it away until the time was right. They were going to offer it to me as a last resort.

Dad's heart must have splintered into a million pieces when he handed over the Thai baht.

Yet he couldn't find the courage to go through with it. He dumped the unopened packet in a garbage bin outside Bangkok airport the morning they departed. That's why Dad was so ashamed. As far as he's concerned, he didn't have the guts to help his daughter when she needed him most.

I never even knew they'd tried. I just assumed Una was holidaying solo, as she often did. I thought Dad was at Nevercloud, as he often was. I don't know how I know all this now, but I do. They never told me a thing.

I realise now why Una was in my dad's office last night. It had nothing to do with any love letter. She was reimbursing him for the return flight to Bangkok. My first guess was spot on; I should have trusted my gut.

Mum didn't know anything about Bangkok either, as it turns out. At least not at first. If she had she would have gone ballistic and not because she thought it was a waste of money or a con. I don't think she ever accepted my disease either, at least not at first. She honestly believed good old-fashioned home cooking and endless hugs would somehow pull me through.

And when that failed, when my muscles continued to waste away and I could no longer make it up the stairs, she did the only thing she could do. She turned practical. She cleared out her old sewing room, invested in an electric bed, and moved me to the ground floor. She made it cosy enough, filling it with scented candles and fresh flowers and even dangling a new dream catcher from the light fitting, hoping that would help. But I didn't want to be there. I didn't want any of that.

So I approached Peter.

I wish now that I hadn't. I wanted to end my life on *my* terms, in *my* own home, in *my own damn bed*. And I wanted to do it safely, with my loved ones close by. The problem is, euthanasia is illegal in most of Australia, so is assisted suicide, yet I needed assistance. I couldn't do it alone.

So I turned to Peter. He's so worldly; he'd have the answers, and it turns out that he did. We sourced our own Nembutal on the dark web just a few weeks ago, Paul watching on, worried, his usual hesitant self, me giggling like it was a joke and isn't this hilarious!

I honestly thought I had the perfect plan. I thought I was so damn clever. I'd pass away with love and celebration in the air, not the whiff of morphine in a cold, clinical hospital bed. I'd do it with my friends and family around. Everyone, that is, except Mum. Oh how I would have loved her by my side, but I knew she'd never accept this and I couldn't do it sneakily with her in the house. She hadn't taken her eyes off me since the diagnosis. She'd catch me, she'd get my stomach pumped, she'd ruin everything.

That's why I encouraged her to accompany Dad to Dubbo this time even though she was fretting about me, and why I agreed to the party when Una suggested it, even though the only two people who knew about my plan were my brothers. I hadn't even let Tessa or Roco in on it. I just wanted them to be happy when I departed; I just wanted them to be their drunken, crazy selves.

The boys and I had it all arranged. Everything had been agreed.

I'd spend one final night with my dearest friends, the people I loved most before I slipped off this mortal coil. It's such a pity Una had to go and turn it into *The Hangover 4*, inviting everybody and their kids, but I was still determined to do it.

The plan was simple enough. I could still pull it off.

As soon as the revellers were drunk enough, my brothers would bring out the cake to corral them by the pool, and then they would secretly carry me upstairs. I would slip into my old bed and then slip away quietly, the tablets washed down with some *Veuve Clicquot*, my beloved siblings holding me tight, sending me off with love and well wishes.

Then everything went to pot.

Peter is wrong to blame himself. I decided against the Nembutal soon after Paul called in with his lame sick kid excuse and long before Peter scurried off to Central Station, tail between his legs. I already knew, even before the cake came out, that I couldn't take those drugs. It was too risky; it would take too long.

I knew the chances of being left to die in peace were slim. Nobody cared about cake. There were too many people running up and down the stairs, there were kids sneaking about, and Una was following my parents' orders and watching me like a hawk, their new iPhone number tucked away in her baggy linen pocket. Just in case.

But that wasn't the main reason I abandoned the plan.

I couldn't do it to Peter. He'd ordered the illegal drugs. They had his digital fingerprints all over them, and if a curious cop bothered to investigate, they'd be sourced straight back to his laptop, to his credit card. I'd seen enough of the news to know that assisting the dying is as good as killing them yourself. I couldn't let him take the fall for me, and I couldn't be sure he'd get off.

That all came to me in a sober rush as I watched my friends get increasingly intoxicated while I sipped Arabella's nonalcoholic virgin margaritas, tears streaming down my face. Today was not the day that I was going to die.

And then I got that text.

If only I hadn't got that text.

CHAPTER 30

The cranky middle-aged neighbour is called Lance, the one with the frisky dog. I remember him well now. He was a single dad, had a son called Timothy, a beautiful teenage boy who died of leukaemia about ten years back. I'm embarrassed to admit I never really got to know either of them. Tim was a few years younger. Lance just seemed so damn sad all the time.

Mum befriended him, though, of course she did. She cooked him endless casseroles and looked in on him before and after. So when I got my diagnosis, I guess he returned the favour. I guess that's why he was wearing that beanie we saw earlier, the same one on Paul's kids' heads. It's got FIGHTMND stitched across the front. All proceeds from the sale go towards finding a cure for motor neurone disease. I was too preoccupied with my own crap to really notice or to thank him for his donation. But I bet Mum did, and I bet she gave him her mobile number before she left for Dubbo and asked him to keep an eye out.

That's the reason he texted her in Dubbo, worried about the party, not because of the noise, not really. He was more concerned about my health. He didn't think it was doing me any good.

And it's the reason he came to the door that night. I remember now. I agreed with him wholeheartedly. It *was* all a bit much. I was feeling very drained, suddenly very weary. I'd already abandoned my suicide pact, and it was time to clear the place out. I thanked him, I turned back, and *that's* when I saw the light on in Dad's study. That's when I wandered in and spotted the small child on tippy-toes, reaching for Dad's gun.

I smiled.

Yes, I remember it distinctly. I was smiling.

I wasn't worried, not one bit. The kid was a good two feet from reaching the firearm; he never even got close.

"Naughty, naughty," I called out, gently scooping him up and sending him on his way, then I turned back, I thought about it for, oh, three seconds, then I reached for the gun myself.

I remember holding it in my hands, just as Dad had done the day I walked in on him. But it was the future I was weighing up, not the past. It suddenly seemed like the perfect solution, one simple way to end my suffering without causing the suffering of others. One quick, unequivocal death, and no one could bring me back and no one would get the blame. No one, of course, but me.

I lived my life in control, and I would finally control how it ended. Gramps had taught me how to shoot when I was twelve, just as he'd taught my brothers, as though preparing me for this very moment. So I knew how to work a firearm, but first I had to check there were bullets, and it didn't take long to find some. They'd been shoved to the back of a bottom drawer, the box old and faded. It felt like a sign to me, a green light from above.

So I quickly shut the office door, I sat down at Dad's desk, and I got to work. I had a new plan, better than the last, or at least that's what I thought.

First I typed a quick farewell on my Facebook page.

It's been fun guys. Love you all. Good night.

Nothing too cheesy, nothing too alarming, although Jan was clearly alarmed when she stumbled upon it while breastfeeding in the dead of night; I hadn't thought of that. I bitterly regret that now.

Then I typed a more private note, this one for Tessa

and Roco. I gave them my blessing. I knew they had chemistry, even before tonight. It's one of the reasons I broke up with Roco last week, even though he thought I was trying to give him a break from my disease, a way out. The truth was we were just biding time, and while my time was running out, he was wasting his.

We had a good relationship, it really was genuine, but Roco only ever latched on to me at that FIGHTMND fundraiser because I looked so damn terrified. Then he stayed with me because, like I said, he's a rescuer, and I needed rescuing, badly.

There was never any future for us, and I should have released him earlier. I should have set him free.

"It's okay, guys," I wrote. "I love you both so much. Please don't spend too long doing 'what's right'—that's just bollocks. You're perfect together, so just get on with it and you'll make me the happiest person alive, well, dead, but you get the drift!"

Then I added a laughing emoji and two red hearts and clicked Send on Facebook messenger. I knew they wouldn't see it for a while; they were still splashing in the pool last time I looked, trying hard not to flirt, pretending not to be madly in love.

Next I looked around for some paper. This note had to be done just right.

That's when I found Mum's light pink stationery sitting on top of Dad's desk. That's also when I noticed the family photo, my favourite picture, the one in Vanuatu. It always made me smile, and I needed more than ever to smile. So I grabbed the frame, I removed the picture, and I tucked it down my jumpsuit. I wanted my family close to my heart. I needed them there for the grand finale.

But I had one last letter to complete.

I took a steadying breath, I jotted the letters D for Dad and M for Mum on that now-infamous pink envelope, and I began to write...

Dear Mum and Dad (Dear Peter, Paul, Jan and the kids),

Please know that I love you all more than life itself, and this is why I choose you, over life. I hope you understand that.

This disease has gone far enough. There is no cure. Let's not kid ourselves. There is no reprieve. And it has left me broken. But I cannot watch it tear you apart as well, and I will not die slowly under your horrified gaze.

There's very little time, and I have to do it while I still have the strength, without implicating anyone else, without any of you here to bear the burden.

I know you're planning to sell Nevercloud, Dad, you think the money will somehow buy me a medical cure, and I love you so much for that. But we all know, deep down, that there is no miracle for me. And while it certainly won't save me, selling your precious land will destroy you and your dreams of ever returning to the place you love most. I won't let you do that. I just won't.

You need to go back there, Dad, and you need to open your heart to that, Mum. It's time. Hell, it's long overdue. If you can't do it for Dad, do it for the boys. They need it just as much as he does.

Please know that I leave with love and joy in my heart. I'm not scared. Not one bit. And I need you to forgive me, because it's the only way forward.

Love, always and forever.
xo Maisie

"And yet you cannot forgive yourself."

This is Neal and he's sitting beside me. He has one mangled arm around me and I feel so secure, so warm and safe.

I cry for some time. I'm not sure how long, but there aren't any tears, not really. It just feels as if I've cried a river.

"But it was my choice," I splutter eventually. "I chose to shoot myself, so why couldn't I remember it? Why did I struggle with that?"

He hugs me tighter. "Most of us regret suicide the second it's done. Most of us don't want to face the fact that we've taken what the world considers the coward's way out, the selfish way out."

I look at him for the first time tonight. Properly I mean, and I say, "You?"

"I slammed my father's Ford Escort straight into a fig tree. Didn't even hesitate. Killed on impact. Destroyed my entire family in the process, and I was the only one in the car."

"Oh God. I'm so sorry."

"Yeah, well, aren't we all?"

"Why?" I ask now, and he shrugs.

"Bullying. Depression. Never feeling like I belonged." He smiles and puts on a silly Welsh accent. "The only gay in the village."

I smile back. I glance around. "And Deseree?"

"Overdose of prescription meds. Most common way for women. She lost her only child a few years back— Serena, she was six-months pregnant. Terrible case of domestic violence. The guy got off with barely a slap. Des never could move past it."

"Oh the poor thing. How horrendous." I feel so terrible about the way I treated her, my smarmy attitude, my mean-spiritedness. "And Emie?" I'm almost too scared to ask.

"Her story's more complicated. Let's just say she slowly starved herself to death."

"Anorexia?"

"Lots of childhood trauma and abuse. Lost the will to eat, to live. Wanted to punish herself."

My eyes close. I gasp. It's all so bloody tragic.

"But it's *not*, don't you see?" says Neal, his tone upbeat. "*Your* death isn't tragic! You were dying anyway, you just put your family out of their misery sooner."

"But how is speeding it up somehow better?"

"Because it put the brakes on all the insanity. You did it to stop your dad from selling his beloved farm and breaking up your family, because you and I both know their marriage would have struggled to survive that."

I'm glancing downwards now, but Neal is not finished yet.

"You did it to stop Peter and Dr Singh from getting accused of manslaughter because, yes, assisted suicide is still illegal in this state."

"*Vijay*?" I'd forgotten about him. I didn't even know the man; how did he become mixed up in all this?

He frowns. "They call him Dr Sleep. He's a euthanasia campaigner and has assisted several suicides in the past, not that they've been able to make anything stick." He sniggers. He's glad of that. "Una brought him in to meet you, see if you were at that stage yet. She didn't know you'd already got hold of some drugs through Peter; she just wanted some advice. Vijay's the one who put the brochures into that green plastic folder and tucked them under your pillow. The ones that fell down the side of your bed. He eventually confessed all to Ruth back at headquarters."

"So that's why he was staring at me all night? That's why he asked me up to my room."

He grins. "That and the fact he's a total sleaze and thought he had a chance."

"*No!*" I say, aghast, and suddenly we're laughing.

And we laugh for some time. It feels so nourishing. We're both buckled over, roaring with hysterics.

Then a thought occurs to me, and I swallow back my laughter. "So why'd he pinch my suicide note?" I say. "My final letter to my family, the one in the pink envelope. Why'd he go and complicate things by removing that? I mean, that put everyone in the clear, including him. The cops would have cleared out a lot earlier if he'd just left it where it was."

"I know!" Neal wipes away happy tears. "He's a sleaze and a meddling twit! Dr Sleep thought Una had written it. Like you, he'd seen her go into your dad's study earlier, during the party, while he and Arabella were sneaking upstairs to have their fun. He didn't realise Una was just dropping off the cash for that flight. He didn't know what she was doing, but then your body was found and everyone was in a flap, and he noticed the letter on the top of your dad's desk while he was calling triple zero. He thought Una must have got a bad case of the truths and was going to incriminate herself or, worse, *him*, so he swiped it during all the chaos. He didn't get a chance to really look at it until much later. That's when he realised it was your suicide note and asked Una to give it to your family."

"Oh how decent of him," I say, snidely. "And the cash?"

"Yep, again, he thought it could be incriminating, so he stuffed that down the couch before the cops got there."

"Meddling fool," I say, then I almost blush. "I can't believe I thought Una and my Dad… Well, I can't believe I even entertained the idea!"

"Hate to break it to you, honey."

"Sorry?"

"Well they *were* stuck in a hotel in Bangkok together, remember?"

I stare at him, the colour draining from my face, and he laughs again. "Don't worry, nothing happened! Your Dad was a total gentleman, so you can wipe that look of horror from you face. He might be a flirt, but he's all show, your old man. Still quite fond of your mum, despite everything. But don't think the thought didn't cross *Una's* mind."

"Oh stop it!" I give him a metaphorical slap. "You're a troublemaker!"

"And you're a good person, Maisie. So stop beating yourself up so much."

I scoff. I know what he's saying, but I don't quite believe him and something still doesn't add up.

"So why didn't I remember?" I ask. "If I was so gallant and brave and really did shoot myself to protect my loved ones, why did I hide the truth from myself for so long?"

His face clouds over. He's not laughing anymore. "It's like I told you before, Maisie. Most of us regret suicide the second it happens. For you—and me, as it turns out—we regretted it the second *before*. Just as you squeezed that trigger, just before the bullet was released, you wished you weren't doing it, and *that's* why you hid the truth from yourself."

I look at him blankly.

"Rule #2, remember?"

I still look puzzled, and he glances at the tunnel, then back. "You really had trouble with that one, didn't you?"

"Come on, Neal, it's been a very long day."

He smiles and I see the Rules of Death have materialised in his hand. He points to the second rule and says, *"Thou shalt not see what the living do not wish thee to see.* Your *living* self did not want your dead spirit to see what you'd done. Despite everything, despite your best intentions, you *did* regret it, Maisie, you *were* ashamed, so you blocked it from yourself. It was too hard to face. It's taken us quite some time to pull it out of you, hasn't it?"

"Yeah. Sorry about that."

"Oh, don't mention it! I was almost as bad. Poor Des had such a hard time of it with me. She kept showing me the absence of brake marks in front of the fig, the lack of vehicles in the vicinity, the weather report—it was a bright and sunny day. No reason to crash; yet I kept searching for a reason, searching for a culprit, someone else to blame. Des couldn't exactly *tell* me what I'd done. It wasn't her place, you see. Rule #4?"

Again I stare at him blankly, and again he glances towards the tunnel, but this time he sniggers and I'm not sure who or what he's sniggering at. *"Thou shall see all when thou is open to seeing,"* he chants. "I wasn't open for many hours. You, well, you were a closed book for almost twenty-four."

I shake my head at myself and I sigh. I get it now.

Now it makes sense. I thought I was being the brave one, opting out early. But *they* were the brave ones, my family, willing to sell their precious possessions and travel to foreign countries and put their freedom on the line, or in my mother's case, just pad my nest, hold me tight and watch me die. How agonising that would have been for her, for all of them, but they were willing to do it. I was the coward. I couldn't bear to see their agony, to witness their pain. I was the cop-out.

"You loved them, Maisie. How many times do I have to tell you that? You thought you were doing the right thing. You have to stop beating yourself up over it."

"Or shooting myself in the head?"

He smiles. "Or that."

I breathe in now, a deep, settling breath, then I turn to him and repeat Jan's question. "So what happens now?"

"Ah, this is the best bit! I love this bit!" His face has lit up like the Sydney Harbour Bridge on New Year's Eve, but it dims considerably when I still look puzzled. "You gave your life for them, now you get something in return. Yes?"

"I do?"

"Oh. My. God!" He turns back to the tunnel, and this time he yells out, "You owe me a fiver, Emie!" Then he turns to my startled expression and says, "I *knew* you didn't read all the rules properly. We had a wager going. I said you wouldn't get past #4, she was sure you'd get right to the end, to that last one. That's the one almost everyone gets fixated on, especially these days. It's an instant gratification thing. Most deadies want their gift before they do all the hard yakka."

"What gift? I don't even know what you're talking about," I say, adding, "And you guys *bet* on me?"

"Sorry, darls, but we had to do *something* to while away the time." He produces the Rules of Death again and points to the final one.

Rule #7. Thou shall be granted one final wish upon entering the light.

"When you see, once you see, you get a final wish," Neal says as if it needed interpreting. "And I think it's safe to say you have *finally* opened your eyes. Hallelujah! So, you get anything you want, honey, just name it."

I smile. I know. I glance down at my house, and I sense that it has already started.

EPILOGUE

It's just as I expected. There is not a cloud in the sky. I chuckle. Hell, I laugh uproariously. I would have been bitterly disappointed if it was raining.

I hear the rumble of a motor, and I watch as Paul's family drives up the gravel road, pulling short just on the other side of a wallaby-proof fence and a rickety old gate with a letter box beside it. It's an old milk can with the word *Nevercloud* scribbled across the front.

A young child jumps out. It's Toby. He's grown two inches.

"I'll get it! I'll get it!" he squeals, racing to unlatch the gate.

He then stands aside as Paul pulls the car across the cattle grills and stops at the other side so Toby can latch it back up and jump back in.

Within minutes they are rumbling down the dusty road towards the old homestead. I can see it's had a fresh lick of paint, and there are newly planted rosebushes out the front. There haven't been roses there since Grandma's day.

I watch as first Mum and then Dad and then, most surprising of all, Peter appears from inside the timber house. I barely recognise Pete. He has a battered Akubra on his head, and is that a plaid belt around moleskin trousers? He used to mock Dad's old country uniform, now he looks every inch the part. He has abandoned the slick suits and dinner shirts, and his hair is overgrown, his face partially covered in a thin, reddish beard. He looks more handsome than he ever has.

They all wave happily as Paul pulls up in front of the house.

"So yer Dad finally won the toss, hey?" This is Gramps and he is chuckling beside me.

"Poor Mum," I say. "How is she coping?"

"Better than you'd think. I even spotted her whipping up some scones the other day. I wasn't sure she even knew how to bake."

"Now, now, Grandpa, Mum's a terrific cook. We're just not all masterchefs like Grandma." The smell of pumpkin scones wafts from somewhere. I don't know if it's Mum's cooking or if it's coming from Forever.

"I still can't believe she gave up her beloved Sydney."

"Oh, they have an apartment there now, she still gets plenty of smog to keep her happy," says Gramps, "and, well, you did sort of ruin the family house didn't you, love? Your folks never could go back into that study." He offers me a warm smile. "Don't beat yourself up though, a change is as good as a holiday. It's done their marriage a whopping great service, and as for Peto, well, he's like a new man."

"I can see that! I can't believe he went with them. I can't believe he gave up London."

"I can't believe he stayed in London for so long. Why do you think he was so miserable?"

"But I never knew he was miserable. Life seemed to be one big party for Peter: whopping salary, flash hotels, a different girl every night."

He snickers. "I rest my case. You're young, love, you don't get it. But people only party like that to hide the misery they feel alone. It's also the reason he never spent much time at home, because your dad knew this, could see it in his eyes. And it's hard to have someone reflect your lie back at you no matter how much you've convinced yourself you're happy."

He sighs, smiles. "Your death woke him up, love; it's just as you wished. Your death saved all of them in a hundred small ways."

"Are they okay?" I ask. "I mean, really okay?"

"They will be. Well, most of the time." Then he shrugs. "They're still human, Maisie. They still fight and fret and carry on. They still miss you terribly, bitterly at times, but they were going to miss you anyway, right? That was always a given. Now they get to miss you free of guilt and you get yer wish, love. They've survived your suicide, and they will keep surviving. At least for a good long while." Then he nods a head downwards. "And at least the old homestead gets some new life, hey?"

My brow furrows. "I'm sorry," I say.

"What for, love?"

"For sticking you in that god-awful urine-scented hellhole."

"Autumn Lodge? Did it smell of urine? I don't remember that." He cackles. "One of the perks of old age, you lose most of your senses. Not such a bad thing."

"Oh, Gramps," I begin, but he waves me off.

"It wasn't so bad, Maisie. Better than being stuck in the middle of all that dust all on my lonesome, just begging the gods to let it rain."

"Really?" I think he's just saying all that to make me feel better, but now he frowns.

"Sure, at least I had company in town. There was a nice group at the Lodge, went to school with half of them, babysat the other half. I can tell you, that Betsy O'Reilly really blossomed. Pity I was so decrepit by the time I got there, or I could've given her a good—"

"Grandpa!" I interrupt him, glancing back towards the tunnel, hoping Grandma didn't hear, and he laughs at me now.

"You young'uns," he says. "You think you're the only ones with blood pumping through your veins."

"Hey, my blood didn't pump for very long, so don't start giving me a hard time."

He gives me a wink instead. "Come on, that *is* your Grandma back there. She's on the last batch of scones for the day, and I'm not missing out like last time."

"Can I stay a little longer? Do you think that's okay?"

He shrugs. "Stay as long as you need; it's part of the program. Just remember Neal is a pig and he's probably already scoffed the lot."

"Ahh let him have my share. I think I owe him that."

He smiles and heads towards the tunnel when he remembers something and turns back. "Oh and Deseree said to tell you there's another one coming in a few minutes if you're up for it."

I glance at Gramps, an eyebrow raised.

"Gunshot victim, just fifty-five. You might relate." Then he sighs sadly and adds, "And if you don't, I can help you out. He was a farmer, from Western Australia. Bank just took his property. The bastards."

"Oh no," I say and he shrugs.

"Don't worry, those bank managers will get their comeuppance."

Then he cackles again as he continues to the tunnel.

"Thanks, Gramps," I call after him, thinking of the incoming spirit. Just one more chaperone job and I have all my points.

Deseree explained it to me once. She's in charge of the program. I think it helps restore her spirit as much as our own.

"Everybody who commits suicide has to assist two other suicide victims across," she said. "It used to be one, but there are too many suicides today, sadly. The Catholics used to say they'd end up in hell, but really, we've already been to hell. Most of us were living it for years; it's the reason so many of us do it."

I know what she means. "But why us?" I asked. "Why other suicides? Aren't we too screwed up?"

"We know more than anyone what drove them to such drastic measures. These are the souls who need extra attention, extra care."

"Is that what Neal was doing?" I said, half smiling.

"You needed Neal," she told me, "and frankly he needed you too. You helped each other across."

"My turn! My turn!"

Toby's voice pulls my attention back to the present, back to the living, and I watch now as Peter lifts his nephew onto a mottled grey gelding, in front of his big sister, Meg, who is beaming from ear to ear like she's just won the lottery, and I guess owning your own pony *is* the tweenie girl's equivalent. The rest of the family are watching, smiling. Paul has an arm slung around Jan. Mum is holding baby Ruby who has doubled in size, and Dad is standing behind young Jack, the boy's head lost inside his own giant Akubra.

They look the picture of happiness, a wholesome family unit, but I know better. I know what Gramps was saying. I know times have been tough and will continue to be tough, that Mum still weeps for me in the middle of the night, and Dad stares at old photos of me, his throat choked up, like he can will me back to life. He's removed all the guns from the property and has hung up family portraits instead. Not the one I pinched, however. They put it back where I wanted it, resting against my heart, then buried me in a deep plot at the edge of Nevercloud, next to Grandma, Gramps, Uncle Bob and several of those naughty cattle dogs I mentioned earlier. I have one of them up here now. He's a hoot. I renamed him Kasper and have given him to Timothy. He's such a sweet kid. I'm keeping him company for Lance. I think he'd appreciate it.

But back to the living, back to Paul and Jan. I know they're still stuck in that tiny shoebox in Chatswood, but they've weighed up their options and have decided they'd rather earn less and have more quality time with their kids. Life is short. I've taught them that.

As for Tessa and Roco? I don't know what happened to them, that's not part of the deal, but I hope they're doing okay. I really do. I hope they're moving on together and having lots of chubby kids and cooking tasty curries and moussaka and keeping Tammie company, just as I hope that Una has settled down with a decent, single guy, and Jonas has grown the hell up, and Leslie and Arabella and all my other friends are still smiling and partying and enjoying their lives, because what's the point otherwise?

What I know for sure is this: my family is okay. And they will continue to be okay. I got my wish, and I am grateful for that.

Eventually, full to flowing with love and joy and just a hint of sadness, I finally pull the silly tiara from my head and turn back towards the tunnel. I will miss them all so dreadfully, but it's time to leave the living and move on with the next stage.

Besides, I want to grab one of Grandma's famous scones. I know a disgruntled farmer who will soon be needing one.

"Hey, Neal!" I call out. "Leave a few for me, mate. Oh and pop the kettle on! We're going to need some tea, some hugs and some good old-fashioned home cooking."

Then I stop and fling the tiara like a Frisbee outwards, watching with delight as the diamantés turn to raindrops and the raindrops fall to earth, and my family cries out with shock and wonder beneath me.

"It's raining! It's raining!" squeals young Toby, and I smile to myself as I head towards the light.

~~~

ACKNOWLEDGEMENTS

First up, I'd like to acknowledge Annie Sarac who edits my books with good humour, great wisdom and endless support. You are such a joy to work with. I'd also like to thank the lovely Elaine Rivers who gives so generously of her time, as well as my sister Michelle and her husband Peter. All four of you are like my personal cheer squad, reading every book I write, catching clumsy errors (not *mine*, surely?), and always lifting me up, reminding me that I'm on the right track. (And I look forward to repaying the favour very soon, Shell!)

Thank you also to my many long-time readers who soak up my stories, follow my blog and subscribe to my newsletter, and a special congratulations to Leslie L. Allen who won my *Name a Character in My New Mystery* competition. She earned the right to have her name used in this book, and while my character bears no resemblance to the *real* Leslie, I thank her from the bottom of my heart for being such a great sport.

On a more serious note: I cannot claim to be an expert on degenerative diseases or suicide, and I apologise, profusely, for any inadvertent errors. They are completely my own. I do have personal experience with both, however, and this book is for those beautiful souls who've headed off to the light well before their time. I hope you've settled in back there and are finally at peace.

In particular, I'd like to acknowledge Charlie and his beloved partner Edwina. MND may have taken your body, Charlie, but your spirit lingers on.

To find out more about Motor Neurone Disease or give a much-needed donation:
- MND Australia: www.mndaust.asn.au/
- The ALS Association: www.alsa.org/

For information on suicide and mental health:
- Beyond Blue: www.beyondblue.org.au

ALSO BY C.A. LARMER

Blind Men Don't Dial Zero
(Sleuths of Last Resort 1)

POLICE say the case is open-and-shut: The heir to a massive fortune slaughters his parents, confesses to the crimes, then turns the gun on himself. His grandfather says, "Not so fast." With the case now closed, Sir George assembles his own crack team of detectives—five amateur sleuths with a nose for mystery and a need to prove themselves—then pits them against each other to solve it.

"This is a fantastic read! lots of twists and turns and a real page turner! Quirky, interesting and complex characters fill this interesting adventure! I loved the book!"
Charlene @Amazon

"Will have even the most seasoned sleuth baffled as these amateurs tackle a wealthy family, loyal employees, and unsavoury boyfriends. You will find this action-filled journey unforgettable and hard to put down"
Peggy Jo Wipf for Readers' Favorite

Killer Twist (Ghostwriter Mystery 1)

KILLER TWIST is the first stand-alone mystery in the popular 'amateur sleuths' series featuring gutsy ghostwriter Roxy Parker and her motley mates.

"Roxy is a compelling character and I couldn't help but adore her. She's 30, hip, very inquisitive, and fiercely independent. A great cozy."
Rhonda @Amazon

"A fun read ... an easy style ... Lots of local flavour."
Parents' Little Black Book @ Amazon

calarmer.com

www.ingramcontent.com/pod-product-compliance
Lightning Source LLC
Chambersburg PA
CBHW031248120726
47905CB00002B/751